"I love you," said the Prince,
"and I am asking you to marry me."

"I am deeply honoured," replied Ina, "but as I have already told you, I am to marry the Marquis."

"The Marquis is not in love with you, but with your aunt. Can you be so blind as not to realise it?"

"That is not true!" denied Ina, but her words were only a whisper. She began to remember things she had not thought of before, and with a convulsive movement of her body she struggled free of the Prince's restraining hands and ran away from him, faster than she had ever run before.

BARBARA CARTLAND

8
THE HORIZONS OF LOVE

A JOVE BOOK

First Jove edition published December 1980

10 9 8 7 6 5 4 3 2 1

Printed in the United States of America

Jove books are published by Jove Publications, Inc., 200 Madison Avenue, New York, NY 10016

Barbara Cartland, the world's most famous romantic novelist, who is also an historian, playwright, lecturer, political speaker and television personality, has now written over 290 books and sold over 150 million books.

She has also had many historical works published and has written four autobiographies, as well as the biographies of her mother and that of her brother, Ronald Cartland, who was the first Member of Parliament to be killed in the last war. This book has a preface by Sir Winston Churchill.

She has recently completed a novel, *Love at the Helm*, with the help and inspiration of the late Earl Mountbatten of Burma, Uncle of His Royal Highness Prince Philip. This is being sold for the Mount-batten Memorial Trust.

Miss Cartland, in 1978, sang an Album of Love Songs with the Royal Philharmonic Orchestra.

In 1976, by writing twenty-one books, she broke the world record and has continued for the following three years by writing twenty-four, twenty-one, and twenty-three.

She is unique in that she was one and two in the Dalton List of Best Sellers, and one week had four books in the top twenty.

In private life Barbara Cartland, who is a Dame of the Order of St. John of Jerusalem, Chairman of the St. John Council in Hertfordshire and Deputy President of the St. John Ambulance Brigade, has also fought for better conditions and salaries for Midwives and Nurses.

As President of the Royal College of Midwives (Hertfordshire Branch) she had been invested with the first badge of Office ever given in Great Britain, which was subscribed to by the Midwives them-selves. She has also championed the cause for old people, had the law altered regarding gypsies, and founded the first Romany Gypsy Camp in the world.

Barbara Cartland is deeply interested in Vitamin Therapy and is President of the British National Association for Health. She has a Health and Hap-piness Club in England.

Her book *The Magic of Honey* has sold through-out the world and is translated into many languages.

She has a magazine, *Barbara Cartland's World of Romance*, now being published in the U.S.A.

AUTHOR'S NOTE

At the end of the nineteenth century and into the beginning of the twentieth, a new way of behaviour for society was known as the Eleventh Commandment. This was —"Thou shalt not be found out."

As I have described in this book a lady entertained her admirer at tea time when her husband was at his Club and was expected to stay there until it was time to dress for dinner.

Girls badly educated and kept in the background were not asked to stay in smart house parties but were married off as quickly as possible.

After a young married woman had been faithful to her husband for about ten years and produced an heir, it was considered reasonable for her to have a discreet *affaire de coeur* as long as the Eleventh Commandment was strictly observed.

Chapter One

1878

"IT IS absolutely ridiculous!" Lady Wymonde said in a sharp voice.

At the same time she looked very lovely as she spoke, although her husband, scowling at the letter he held in his hand, did not notice.

Lord Wymonde, who was getting on for forty-five, was beginning to lose the trim figure he had when he was younger.

He was, however, still an excellent horseman and an acknowledged hard rider in the hunting-field.

"It is no use arguing, Lucy," he said. "Either we take Ina with us to Chale, or we do not go!"

"Now you are being absurd," Lady Wymonde said angrily. "How can I ask Alice to have an unfledged Schoolgirl in the kind of party she has arranged at Chale? You know as well as I do that your tiresome niece will be out of place."

"Nevertheless she is my niece," Lord Wymonde said, "and that means you will have to chaperon her for the rest of the Season and see that she is invited to all the Balls."

Lady Wymonde stamped her foot.

"It is intolerable that at thirty I should be a chaperon. I want to be dancing myself, not trying to find partners for some gauche and unattractive girl."

They both knew she was thirty-six last birthday, but great beauties were traditionally ageless and Lady Wymonde was undoubtedly one of the most outstanding beauties in London.

She would, in fact, have said she was less than thirty, but their son Rupert was twelve and as he was already at Eton it was impossible to make him out to be any younger.

Lord Wymonde folded the letter and put it into his pocket.

"As the post has been delayed owing, I imagine, to the inefficiency of the French," he said, "Ina will be arriving tomorrow."

"Tomorrow?" Lady Wymonde's voice rose in a shriek.

Almost gasping for breath, she added:

"And you expect me, when I will not have a moment to myself all day, to meet her and make her respectable enough to go to Chale on Friday?"

"As I have already suggested, we can stay at home," Lord Wymonde answered, "but doubtless your host would miss you."

2

There was a note of sarcasm in his voice which Lady Wymonde noticed and it checked the angry words that were already forming on her lips.

George was an easy-going and on the whole a complacent husband, but she knew she dare not push him too far, for where his family pride was concerned, he could be very difficult.

That was why he was making a fuss about his niece, and Lucy could think of nothing more infuriating at this moment, when she was engaged in one of the most exciting and thrilling *affaires* she had ever known, to be landed with a young girl.

She disliked girls, she always had. It was not only because they had the one thing no amount of money could buy, which was youth, but they also undoubtedly were restrictive in a house party that was chosen for its sophistication and wit.

She knew only too well what a party at Chale entailed, and as this one was being given particularly for her she had been very careful in her choice of the Marquis's other guests.

"I want you at Chale," he had said the other evening when they were sitting out at a Ball given by the French Ambassador.

It was always difficult to talk privately, and even when the Marquis called on Lucy in the afternoons when George was at his Club, there were few times when she could contrive that no one else would be present.

"You know how much I want to talk to you alone," he added.

Lucy allowed a small smile to part her exquisitely curved lips.

She knew exactly what he meant by "alone." He wanted to kiss her and, Heaven knows, she wanted that and a great deal more.

She glanced at him from under her eyelashes and thought that never in all her years as an outstanding success had there ever been a man so attractive as the Marquis of Chale.

Usually Lucy was quite content to be admired, to be paid compliments, and know that men were frustrated by her indifference which only made them desire her the more.

"You drive me mad! You are so cold and cruel," they would say passionately. "How can I make you love me?"

How often Lucy had heard this and how often had she replied:

"You know I am fond of you, but . . ."

There had always been that "but," and if a man became too ardent, Lucy, while enjoying every moment of it, would always say wistfully:

"I have to be careful. George is very jealous."

But with the Marquis everything had been different.

First of all she had sought him out.

The mere sight of him walking into the Ballroom looking so tall and so handsome, so imperious and at the same time so bored, had made her feel very different from the way she had ever felt about a man before.

When they danced together she had known he was mildly interested in her looks, but there was nothing specially eager in the way he put his hand on her small waist.

She had been well aware as they moved on the dance-floor that his heart was not beating any quicker, while hers was behaving in a very unusual manner.

It had taken two months before he made the first overtures, and during that time she had almost despaired.

She tried every wile to intrigue and arouse him, but she had the feeling that he saw through all the little manoeuvres that had captured other men, and knew them for what they were.

Then at last, when Lucy was almost desperate, he had kissed her one afternoon when they were alone in her Drawing-Room at tea time, and it had ignited between them a flame that began to burn more brightly every time they met.

To Lucy it was a revelation because those who had found her cold were entirely right in their supposition.

She was a cold woman, interested only in herself and her beauty, and not moved by anyone's suffering, except her own.

But with the Marquis it was different, and because she knew agonisingly that he was six years younger than she was, she scrutinised her face in the mirror, looking for every tiny line that might become a wrinkle, for every surplus ounce on her beautiful body which might be the forerunner of middle-age.

"I am young, I am young!" Lucy told herself every morning.

She felt as if she could will her body into the lissom slenderness she had had when she was seventeen and had left the schoolroom to find to her astonishment that she was beautiful.

Her fame had not, of course, come overnight. She had to wait a year until she was married to George.

It was then as Lady Wymonde that she had taken Society by storm.

She learnt to dress, she learnt to say amusing things in her obviously contrived musical voice.

Most of all, she realised that by looking beautiful and cold she made men flock to her side, determined with a conceit which existed in every one of them, that they would melt the "Ice Maiden."

They failed and Lucy had begun to believe that she was, in fact, apart from most women who admitted in the secrecy of their Boudoirs that love was something they yearned for and desired.

"I hate men who want to touch me and maul me about. I find it extremely tiresome," Lucy had said to her three most intimate friends.

"You cannot be serious!" one of them exclaimed.

"But I am," Lucy insisted. "When I know that a man is in love with me I enjoy the 'swimmy' look in his eyes, but quite frankly, I do not wish him to kiss me."

"Lucy, you cannot be telling the truth!"

"I am."

"Then you are unnatural," a woman who was a little older than the rest said sharply.

Lucy had not minded.

She knew what she wanted and was determined to get it. It was simply to have a position in Society that was unassailable, frequent invitations to Marlborough House, and of course, the knowledge that no party could be a success unless she was there.

Then she had met the Marquis of Chale and he had turned her little world upside-down.

"I suppose this is love!" Lucy said to herself at first incredulously.

Then as the Marquis had proved himself to be more elusive than she herself had ever been, she knew that the ice was melting and it was a decidedly frustrating sensation.

But she had won! She had won! The Marquis was now pursuing her, and the first major step had been when he said he wanted to give a party at Chale for her.

Of course she had been there before.

Alice, the mother of the Marquis, was an old friend who contrived to make her parties a success by inviting distinguished, rich, and famous men with the most beautiful women in England as entertainment.

The mixture was sufficient to ensure that anyone who was asked to Chale considered it a privilege, apart from the fact that the house itself was fantastic.

It was enormous, comfortable, and made the guests feel as if they had stepped into a Dream Palace where there were a hundred genii waiting to grant them their slightest wish.

"How do you manage to make everything run so smoothly, Alice?" Lady Wymonde once asked the Marchioness.

She had laughed.

"I can tell you in two words, Lucy. Organisation and money!"

It was this sort of remark that invariably evoked screams of laughter and Lucy had thought how she would give anything in the world to be the chatelaine of Chale.

Not that there was any possibility of that happening, unless George had a fatal accident, or apoplexy from drinking too much port.

Even so, Lucy told herself, it would be difficult to make the Marquis marry her.

For one thing she was quite certain he was not the marrying type, although he would have to have a son and heir sooner or later.

But that was something Lucy had no wish to give him, although she thought she might make the effort, if it was a question of marriage.

After Rupert had been born, the heir to the title of which George was exceedingly proud, Lucy had said "No more!"

"I think it important for us to have more than one child," George said.

"Important or not," Lucy had replied, "I have no intention of spoiling my figure."

She had known that George was disappointed, as his first wife who had died five years before he married again, had been unable to have any children.

But Lucy told herself she had done her duty and no man should ask for more especially when his wife was as beautiful as she was.

The Marquis would, of course, want an heir. What man did not hanker after having a son to succeed him?

But Lucy was determined that she would not

think of his marriage, unless it was to herself, for a very, very long time.

'We will be very happy,' she thought reassuringly.

She knew as she glanced at herself in the mirror that no man could ask for anyone more beautiful or more alluring than she was at this moment.

Love had given her face a new radiance. It had also softened her eyes and perhaps her features.

She had always been every man's ideal of an English rose. Her hair was the gold of ripening corn, her eyes the blue of a summer sky, her skin very white. There was just a touch of pink in her cheeks, while her lips, as dozens of men had told her, were made for kisses.

"I am beautiful, beautiful!" Lucy had said when she awoke this morning, "and when I am with the Marquis at Chale then the last barrier between us will fall, and I will have him where I want him— at my feet!"

She preened herself a little in the mirror which reflected her as she sat back against her lace-edged pillows in the large bedroom where the windows overlooked Hyde Park.

"I love you!"

She could almost hear the Marquis saying the words in his deep voice which had the power to move her even when he made the most commonplace remark.

When she rose and dressed with the help of two lady's maids, she felt as if she was moving to music.

And now George had spoilt everything!

Not only was it infuriating to have to take another

guest with her to Chale, but that it should be a young girl made it worse.

It was not a question of her being a rival. It was not that which Lucy feared. It was that Ina would be completely out of place in what was to be *her* party.

And George, instead of paying attention to the attractive Mrs. Marshall whom she had chosen particularly for him, would be dribbling over his niece because she was "family."

Lucy wanted to scream at the annoyance the whole idea was causing her.

Then she remembered that was not the way to manage George.

With an effort she forced herself to walk across the room towards him, put both her hands on the lapels of his coat and look up at him appealingly.

"Please, George, let us make other arrangements for your niece," she begged. "You know how much I am looking forward to being at Chale and in a party that will consist of many of our dearest friends. A young girl would be so out of place."

Because she looked so lovely when she was pleading with him she thought for a moment from the expression in her husband's eyes that he was going to give in to her.

Then he said:

"When we are at Chale you will have your new admirer to run your errands. So tell him to invite someone young to keep Ina company."

Now there was a note in his voice that told Lucy that George was jealous and she had been very stupid not to anticipate that he might be so where the Marquis was concerned.

She was aware that George had tolerated with a kind of amused contempt the other men who were quite obviously infatuated with her, but whom she had always kept at arm's length.

She had never imagined that he would be perceptive enough to realize that the Marquis was different.

But now she knew she had underestimated him and she would, in fact, have to be very careful not to upset him so much that he made it difficult for her ever to be alone with the Marquis or even to see him.

She remembered uncomfortably that George had always been very intolerant of the *affaires de coeur* in which practically every one of their friends were deeply engaged.

"The whole palaver is damned undignified, if you ask me!" he had said once.

On another occasion when the scandal about the wife of one of his particular cronies had been the talk of his Club, he had said:

"If she was my wife, I would give her a damned good hiding, take her to the country, and make her stay there!"

Lucy had laughed.

"You sound like a caveman, George! It is out of date to be so primitive."

"A man must protect his good name," George replied.

Looking down at her now, he said:

"I am not going to argue any more, Lucy. We will arrange for Ina to come to Chale with us, or we will all go home. The garden will be looking beautiful at this time of the year."

Lucy knew as he spoke, that he was longing to be at their house in Sussex which was partially closed during the Season.

She had always known that George really disliked London, apart from being able to meet his friends at the Club, or attend the horse-sales at Tattersall's.

He always grew disagreeable when it was time to open their house in Park Lane and take up most of the servants from the country to augment the skeleton staff which was kept in London during the hunting and shooting season.

To Lucy, London was her idea of Heaven and she felt in the country she was wasting precious days, hours and minutes when there were few men to admire her beauty.

She was also well aware that for them a good day's hunting or a "bag" of a thousand pheasants was more attractive than she was.

Because she would have been very foolish if she had not read the danger signals in George's attitude, she said quickly:

"If it means so much to you, dearest, of course Ina must come to Chale. I am sure you will look after her and see she does not feel out of it."

She saw the surprise in her husband's eyes that she was being so amenable, and she gave him a smile that one admirer described as being 'like the sun coming through the clouds on a dark day.'

"I thought you would see sense," Lord Wymonde said a little heavily.

He put his arms round his wife, drew her to him and kissed her cheek.

With an effort she prevented herself from telling

him not to crease her gown and after a second stepped out of his reach.

"You must make all the arrangements about meeting this child," she said, "but I think it is unlikely that we can provide her with any suitable clothes for the occasion, unless she is the same size as I am."

As she spoke Lucy was thinking of the wardrobes filled with gowns that reposed on the second floor.

She had meant for sometime to send a great number of them away to her poorer relations who received a parcel, or sometimes a trunk of Lucy's discarded garments from time to time.

They all wrote enthusiastic letters of thanks which made Lucy feel that she was extremely charitable.

It never struck her for one moment that the cousins she patronised in this manner, were either a good deal older than she was herself, or lived in the wilds of Wales.

They therefore had little or no use for elaborate Ball gowns, cut low and embroidered with diamanté, or creations which had drawn everybody's eyes at Ascot and which, because they had been so outstanding, could not be worn again.

Thinking that problem was disposed of, Lucy went to her desk and sat down to write a letter to the Marquis.

In a secret drawer to which only she had a key, there lay a number of letters written to her over the years, sometimes imploring, sometimes angry and accusing, but there were so far regrettably few from the Marquis.

Because she wanted to see them she took them out and realised as she read them that he had said nothing that George could not have read without suspicion, or anyone else who was interested.

For a moment she felt almost as if she had received a shock.

Then she remembered the Marquis had not written to her since that long kiss which had left them both breathing a little quicker and Lucy's heart thumping in her breast.

"He loves me, and he will love me a great deal more before I have finished!" she told herself reassuringly and started her letter to him.

The Marquis opened it the following day at breakfast.

He noticed vaguely and without very much interest that Lucy's writing-paper was thick and creamy with the Wymonde crest engraved above the address, and that her hand-writing was extremely elegant and the capitals beautifully shaped.

The Marquis read what the letter contained, then when he had finished breakfast went upstairs to his mother's suite.

There was a large Dower House on the estate waiting for the Marchioness when her son married and she relinquished her position as mistress of Chale.

She always said she would enjoy living in the smaller house and not having so many responsibilities.

Actually this was untrue.

The Marchioness had never liked the idea of being relegated to the position of Dowager. Having reigned as Queen, or rather as Empress, over the Kingdom that centred round such a magnificent Palace as Chale, she had no wish to retire.

What was more, like Lucy, the Marchioness wanted to remain young and for very much the same reason.

Alice Chale also had in her youth been a beauty, but unlike Lucy she was dark with perfect features, and her dark slanting eyes gave her an air of mystery which Queen Victoria thought slightly reprehensible.

Men found her irresistible and the young Marchioness of Chale had broken hearts strewn round her which had aroused envy, hatred, and malice in the breasts of all her contemporaries.

She had swept through life, however, with an imperiousness that had made her ignore criticism and find those who disliked her as beneath her notice.

It was only when the Marquis died and her position at Court was not so important as it had been, that she began to realise that she was growing old and there was not such a large circle of admirers as there had been in the past.

They had dispersed because of age and marriage and, although the Marchioness would not care to admit it, they preferred pursuing younger women.

It was also obvious that where before she had had the choice of dozens of lovers, she would now have to concentrate on a chosen few.

These had gradually been whittled down to one man who was prepared to offer her his devotion and live a very comfortable life in the process.

The Marquis thought of them as his mother's "tame cats" and was quite prepared to tolerate them if it made her happy.

To him it was very much the same as her having a lap-dog like a pug or a King Charles spaniel.

He thought that their impact on Chale was rather less than the sporting dogs that he always had at his heels.

The "lap-dog" at the moment who kept the Marchioness company wherever she went was Harry Trevelyn.

A man of nearly forty, he had been a hanger-on of the rich all his life, paying his way by being a near-perfect guest who would do anything asked of him.

He danced well, played a good game of Bridge, was proficient at billiards, and could always be relied on to make himself pleasant to the most disagreeable old Dowager or the plainest woman.

He was also someone to talk to, to rely on, and who never failed to make the Marchioness feel that she was still beautiful.

Because she was determined to remain so, if only in Harry's eyes, she took great care of herself.

For one thing she never appeared at Chale or at any of her son's other houses until, as she said, 'the day was well aired.'

At about noon, exquisitely and expensively gowned, her hair arranged by a skilled lady's maid and her face discreetly made up, she would come downstairs looking very like the portraits of her which were to be found in every room in which her husband had habitually sat during his lifetime.

He had fallen in love with her because she was

beautiful, and to him she had always looked exactly the same as she had when she was seventeen.

She had been married before her eighteenth birthday which was why she was able quite convincingly to declare that fifty was only the youth of old age.

The Marquis knocked on his mother's door in the South Wing which contained the most comfortable and sunny rooms in the house.

It was opened by a lady's maid who curtsied at the sight of him.

"Good-morning, Rose!"

"Good-morning, M'Lord."

The Marquis walked past her into the large bedroom where in the huge bed under a canopy decorated with cupids the Marchioness was reading the newspapers.

She quickly took off her glasses because she hated to be seen in them, and smiled as her son crossed the room to kiss the hand she held out to him.

"Good-morning, Mama!"

"Good-morning, dearest. You are early this morning."

"I am riding out to Ponders End to see the houses I am building there," the Marquis explained, "but that is not what I came to see you about."

"What is it?"

The Marchioness was thinking as she asked the question how handsome her son was and very like his father at the same age.

They were both tall and broad-shouldered and had clear-cut features that were unmistakably English.

Unusually perceptive, for she was not a very

imaginative woman, the Marchioness thought that lately her son had been seeming bored and dissatisfied in a way it was hard to describe.

"Lucy Wymonde wants to bring George's niece with her on Friday."

"Niece!" the Marchioness exclaimed. "I did not know he had one."

Then before the Marquis could reply she added:

"But of course! It must be Roland Monde's daughter."

The Marquis waited, knowing his mother was working it out in her mind and that with her retentive memory, she was better than any *Debrett* or *Who's Who* when it was a question of placing a member of someone's family in the right category.

"Roland died last year when he was living abroad," the Marchioness went on, "and his wife died several years ago. That means the girl is an orphan."

"Lucy speaks as if she is going to live with them," the Marquis said.

His mother laughed.

"Poor Lucy! She will hate that! She has no partiality for girls!"

"I am not surprised."

"And yet," his mother answered, "they soon turn into the beautiful sophisticated women you find so fascinating."

There was no doubt there was an innuendo in her words, and the Marquis laughed.

"Stop teasing me, Mama!" he commanded, "and rearrange the dinner table or get old Wickham to do it for you."

"I will," the Marchioness answered.

They both knew Miss Wickham who had been residential secretary at Chale for years, was far more efficient at arranging the *placement* of the table than she was.

As the Marquis, having said what he had come to say, appeared to be leaving, the Marchioness remarked:

"I know this party is rather important to you, Irvine, but I think George Wymonde might be difficult if he thinks his honour is in any way being jeopardised."

The Marquis looked at his mother in surprise.

She never interfered with any of his love-affairs, or even discussed them.

"I have not the least idea, Mama, what you are talking about," he replied.

"I am only warning you," the Marchioness said. "I am fond of Lucy. I have known her for a great number of years and I thought last week when you were dancing together she looked lovelier than I have ever seen her."

She thought as she spoke there was a glint in her son's eyes, but she could not be certain.

Then as if he felt that she was encroaching on something that did not concern her, the Marquis said:

"I hope both George and Lucy will enjoy themselves. I have received a great deal of hospitality from them, and this party is my way of returning it."

He was on the defensive, and the Marchioness thought it wise to say no more.

When he had left her, she lay back against her pillows with a little sigh.

She loved her son and she knew he ought to marry, even though it would be a blow to her personally to have to leave Chale.

Marriage was one thing; Lucy Wymonde another. The Marchioness had no wish for him to break his heart as quite a number of men had done already because they loved Lucy who loved no one but herself.

'I would hate him to be hurt,' the Marchioness thought.

She knew that if she had been doing her duty long before now, she would have produced the right sort of girls coming from the right families, to make her son the right sort of wife to reign at Chale.

But when the Marchioness thought of being a grandmother, she shuddered.

Then she would really be old, and no amount of cosmetics, expensive gowns, or glittering jewels would hide her age from men like Harry, who always pretended to believe the Marquis was younger than he was.

"A grandmother!"

She gave a frightened cry and picked up the hand-mirror which lay on the sheets beside her, to look at her face in it.

The Marquis was not thinking either of his mother, or of Lucy, or anything else but the horse he was riding.

It was a very spirited stallion which he had acquired only recently, and with which he was having a battle as he rode down the drive.

He had come to Chale yesterday, though he was well aware that he had accepted at least half-a-dozen important invitations in London, simply because he wished to ride this particular horse.

That had seemed to him more inviting at that precise moment even than the chance of seeing Lucy.

He had merely to say to his secretary in London: "I am going to Chale," for the wheels to start rolling and everything was arranged with the perfection which came from long practise.

Now, with the wind on his face, his knees gripping the horse's sides, he felt happy and more excited than he had felt for months.

The stallion was trying every trick he knew to unseat his rider, or to refuse to do what was required of him. But he began to realise almost before they were half-way down the drive, that he had met his master.

As his defiance gradually turned to respect, the Marquis felt an exhilaration at being the victor, that he felt occasionally when a woman surrendered herself for the first time.

The stallion, encouraged by a sharp spur, settled into a somewhat uneasy gallop across the Park.

He was still wondering how he could dislodge the man on his back, but he was beginning to think it was going to be more difficult than he anticipated.

The Marquis was thinking he was extremely glad that he was not in London.

Today he would have to himself and his horses. Not only the stallion he was riding now, he remembered, required his attention but there was another horse he intended to ride this afternoon, which his Head Groom had already informed him was unmanageable.

It constituted a challenge he could not resist.

Tomorrow there was a local race-meeting at which he always gave away the prizes besides having horses running in two races, and the following day the house-party would arrive with Lucy.

For a moment his thoughts lingered on her, thinking how beautiful she was, and the unexpected fire he had aroused in her when they had kissed.

Then the stallion beneath him, as if he knew his thoughts were elsewhere deliberately shied at a fallen tree.

The Marquis's hands tightened on the reins and man and beast were again fighting each other to the intense satisfaction of them both.

Arriving in London on the boat-train from Dover, Ina thanked the elderly couple who had offered her the hospitality of their cabin during the Channel crossing.

She had asked for one when she came aboard and was told they were all engaged.

Because she looked so young and forlorn, the man moving away from the Purser with a cabin number in his hand, glanced at his wife, then said:

"I am afraid we have taken the last cabin available, but if you would like to join us you will be very welcome."

"That is very kind of you," Ina replied. "I should indeed be grateful if I might do so."

The elderly gentleman glanced at his ticket.

"Cabin D."

"I will just see that my maid is comfortably settled down, then I will join you, if I may."

The gentleman raised his hat and with his wife holding onto his arm, they walked slowly to the cabin.

Ina had told them how grateful she was.

"I do not feel sea-sick myself," she said, "unless other people are being sick around me, but my maid loathes the sea and feels sick even to think about it!"

Her new friends had laughed, and now when she said goodbye to them, the gentleman said:

"I hope there will be somebody to meet you at the station."

"I am expecting my uncle," Ina said, "because I am sure my aunt will be too busy."

"Is your aunt the beautiful Lady Wymonde?" the old gentleman enquired.

"I have never seen her, but I have heard that she is very, very lovely," Ina replied.

"She is indeed," the gentleman smiled. "She is always described in the newspapers as being the most beautiful woman in England, and that is what I thought when I saw her at the opening of Parliament."

"We were not present of course in the House of Lords," the Lady explained quickly, as if she thought

23

Ina might think her husband was boasting, "but because we were curious, we watched the Peers and Peeresses arrive in their carriages, and in their diamonds and robes they were truly magnificent!"

Ina's eyes shone.

"You make it sound very exciting!"

"That is exactly what it was," the Lady said, "but you will be able to have a close-up view of Lady Wymonde. You are lucky!"

"Yes, I am," Ina replied.

She spoke in all sincerity.

At the same time she could not help remembering how her father had laughed at the social life lived by his brother and sister-in-law.

"Scrabble, scrabble, up the ladder, to seize the gaudy baubles of social acclaim," he had said derisively. "That life is not for me, Ina, or for you. It is false and foolish."

But now, Ina thought, that was the life she would be living in the future if, as she was afraid, she was to become part of her uncle and aunt's household.

And yet, what else could she do except come back to England after Mrs. Harvester had died?

The train came into Victoria Station and looking through the window a little anxiously, Ina was certain that she recognised her uncle, even though as far as she could remember, she had never seen him before.

Her father had always said there was a Wymonde likeness that was inescapable.

"Whether he likes it or not, George and I look alike, although we certainly do not think alike."

Because her uncle looked so like her father whom

she had loved, Ina felt a little catch in her throat as the train drew to a standstill and a porter opened the door.

She could see the man she had identified standing looking around him a little way from her. He was very smart, with a top hat at a dashing angle on his head, and a carnation in his buttonhole.

With a last goodbye to her kind friends, she hurried down the platform knowing that Hannah would collect everything she had left behind and come after her.

She had travelled in the next carriage and refused firmly to go First Class.

"The right and proper place for me, Miss Ina, is Second," Hannah said, "and now you are starting a new life with your uncle and aunt, we'll start off on the right foot, you and me, and that means I'm a lady's maid and nothing more, and don't you forget it!"

"Lady's maid or not, I love you, Hannah!" Ina said, "and all these years, since Mama died, if you had not looked after me, I should have been in a nice mess, and you know it!"

"That's as maybe!" Hannah said sharply, "but I know what's best and I'm not having people telling me my place because I've stepped out of it!"

Ina had known that Hannah was right. At the same time, she felt her heart sink at the thought of what lay ahead.

She had lived a very different life with her father in many strange parts of the world where he had settled for seldom more than a year, when he wanted to paint a particular landscape or its people.

Then without very much notice they would move on somewhere else, simply because he thought it would be more attractive.

To Ina the countries they visited were fascinating, but she was well aware how lost and indeed unhappy she would have been without Hannah when her father had not only the attraction of painting, but other attractions as well.

Sometimes he would disappear for weeks on end and Ina had no idea where he had gone or what he was doing.

If Hannah knew she would not say, but merely strove to keep Ina from being too curious and to ensure that she concentrated on her lessons.

"Papa does not mind if I am clever or not," Ina said once.

"That's what you think," Hannah had retorted. "He'd soon get bored if you were ignorant like some of those women he uses as models, with nothing to say for themselves except to hold out their hands for money."

Ina's eyes had sparkled, and after that she had worked hard because she thought that what she learnt would please her father.

He had often talked to her in the evenings as if she was a woman of his own age, and she began to understand that this was a compliment and she gave him something that was lacking in his life.

He was a clever man and while sometimes he brought men to the house to whom Ina would listen with interest, she had no idea who the majority of his friends were or what they were like.

All she really knew was that when a place had

no more to give him from the point of view either of his painting or of the people with whom he associated, they moved on.

When he had died last year she could hardly believe it had happened.

He had complained of a pain in his chest for about two months, but he refused firmly to see a doctor saying, when Hannah asked him to do so, that he was only suffering from indigestion.

Then one morning when his valet went to call him he was lying across the bed as if he had fallen on it and had died from a heart attack.

"He must have been in quite considerable pain from time to time," the doctor told Ina.

She thought it was typical of her father that he would not give in to any weakness, and would rather suffer than be what he called "fussed over."

It was then she thought she would have to get in touch with her uncle, but an elderly woman called Mrs. Harvester, who lived in the next villa to the one which her father rented, near Nice, had befriended her.

She had heard from her servants that the Honourable Roland Monde was dead, and immediately had asked Ina to come to her.

Ina had done so by climbing the wall between their two gardens.

When she first called on Mrs. Harvester a year earlier, she soon realised that her Villa was very different from their own untidy, not particularly attractively decorated Villa.

Mrs. Harvester had excellent taste. Her furniture which she had brought, Ina learnt, from a big house in England, consisted of priceless antiques, and the pictures were by famous old Masters which Ina recognised.

Mrs. Harvester was seventy, and lonely.

She had first watched from the window Ina playing in the garden of the Villa next door.

She had made it her business to call on Roland Monde and he found they had a number of friends in common.

"Not that I expect they would remember me," Ina's father had said. "I have not been back to England for years."

"Why not?" Mrs. Harvester asked.

"Because it bores me," he replied. "My family are still doing the same things they have done for generations, while I want fresh horizons and new ideas. England is predictable as Good Friday's sermon!"

Mrs. Harvester had laughed.

She begged Roland Monde to call and see her, but in the end only Ina went because she was fascinated by the things inside the house and the knowledge their owner had of them.

"Tell me about this," she would ask of some huge inlaid *secretaire* or work-box reputed to have belonged to a Queen, long dead.

Mrs. Harvester had stories about everything, and Ina often thought that she was starved of stories which were not the sort that one found in books, but could only be repeated at first hand.

When Mrs. Harvester invited Ina and Hannah to move into her Villa, they had gone thankfully.

They were both aware, although they did not say

so, that it put off the evil hour when they would have to return to England.

When her uncle had written condoling with her over the loss of her father and asking her what she intended to do in the future, and when she had replied that she was staying with a friend, a Mrs. Harvester, who had known her father, he had not suggested that she should make other arrangements.

Then unfortunately Mrs. Harvester had died.

To Ina it seemed impossible that first she should lose her father in such a sudden way, then Mrs. Harvester.

The latter in fact, was ill for three weeks, but even so it had come as a shock, and it was Hannah who had then said firmly that now they must return home to England.

Mrs. Harvester had left some of her treasures to Ina and quite a considerable sum of money.

The rest was claimed by a grandson she had never liked and who had come to Nice determined to dispute aggressively anything that Ina claimed.

When he saw her he changed completely and actually seemed not only resigned, but quite pleased that she should have everything his grandmother had left her.

"Let us get a little house and live here on our own," Ina had pleaded to Hannah.

But the old maid said she knew what was right and what was wrong, and it was right for Ina to go back to her own people.

"You're nearly eighteen, Miss Ina, and it's time you became a débutante and made your curtsy at Buckingham Palace."

"I have no wish to do that, Hannah," Ina said quickly.

"It's the right thing for you to do!" Hannah answered firmly.

It was 'the right thing' to write to her Uncle George. It was 'the right thing' to have her furniture and pictures stored until she could send for them.

It was 'the right thing' to say goodbye to her father's grave in the Cemetery at Nice and, Ina thought, to leave behind the sunshine, the orange trees and the palms.

"At least England will be something new," Ina said wistfully as the train carried her across France.

"It's right you should go back to your own country," Hannah said in an uncompromising voice.

There was silence. Then Ina said in a small voice:

"Do you think . . . Uncle George will be . . . pleased to see me?"

"He's your uncle, and he'll do what's right," Hannah replied.

And that, Ina thought to herself, was cold comfort.

Chapter Two

LORD WYMONDE watching the passengers alight from the train thought the tall, rather attractive young woman wearing brown would be Ina.

Then he saw following her from the carriage there was a man and knew it was unlikely.

He was just considering whether he should speak to another woman who was, he thought with dismay, decidedly plain, when a lilting voice beside him said:

"I am sure you are Uncle George!"

He looked down and saw what he thought must be a child, then realised that the girl speaking to him was older, but still looked almost incredibly young.

She only reached to his shoulder and she had pale blue eyes that had a decided look of excitement in them, and her round hat set back on her head haloed very fair hair, the colour of corn.

Because for a moment Lord Wymonde seemed tongue-tied Ina said:

"I am Ina, and you do look very much like Papa as he told me you would."

"You are Ina!" Lord Wymonde exclaimed rather heavily. "My dear child, I should never have recognised you."

Ina give a little laugh.

"You were not likely to, as you have never seen me, except perhaps in my cradle."

"No, that is true," Lord Wymonde admitted, "but I expected you to look older."

"And of course taller," Ina added smiling. "It is very regrettable, but it does not seem likely that I shall ever grow any higher than I am now."

She said it with a note of mock dismay in her voice and Lord Wymonde was forced to laugh.

At the same time he told himself she was extraordinarily pretty, in fact lovely, and certainly unlike anything he had expected.

"Well, welcome home to England!" he said in a genial manner, "and now we must see to your luggage."

"I think my maid Hannah has gone to the Guard's van," Ina replied.

Looking round she saw Hannah's black bonnet bobbing up and down as she obviously pointed out their trunks to a porter.

"Good!" Lord Wymonde said. "Then we can

leave that to her. I suppose she knows you are staying at Wymonde House?"

"I will just tell her that I am going ahead with you," Ina replied, "or she might worry."

She slipped away as she spoke, and ran in a way Lord Wymonde vaguely thought Lucy would think reprehensible, along the platform.

He could see her in the distance with her face turned up to the elderly woman, talking animatedly.

"She is damned attractive!" he said to himself. "Roland, being an artist, would produce something that might have stepped out of a picture!"

Then he remembered how Lucy had decried his brother's way of life, finding it incredible that he should wish to wander about the world rather than live in the Social World which the Wymondes had adorned for many generations.

As Lord Wymonde thought of it he felt uncomfortably that Lucy would also disapprove of Ina, not for anything she had done, but for the way she looked.

Then he told himself that Lucy's position as a beauty was unassailable.

She could not be so stupid as to be jealous of a girl who had only just left the School-Room, and would obviously have none of the sophistications which were essential to the circle that Lucy embellished so brilliantly.

Girls, of no importance until they were married, were expected to be quiet when older people were present, and as their parents found them unmitigated bores, the sooner they were married off to somebody suitable, the better.

"Lucy will find Ina a husband," Lord Wymonde told himself consolingly as he fancied there might be storms ahead.

When she came running back to him smiling and with a look of excitement in her eyes, he was sure of it.

As they got into the comfortable carriage which was drawn by two horses and had two liveried servants on the box, Ina cried:

"This is very exciting, Uncle George. I have been so looking forward to seeing England and of course, you."

Because it was an unusually warm day, the carriage was open, and as they left the station Lord Wymonde was aware that his niece was sitting forward on the edge of her seat, as if she was afraid she might miss something and looking around her with an enthusiasm he had not seen for years.

"You might have come back when your father died," he remarked.

"As I wrote to tell you," Ina answered, "Mrs. Harvester, who lived in the next Villa to us, asked me to stay with her, and as I had not finished my various classes and the tutors were excellent, I thought it would be a mistake to leave Nice."

Lord Wymonde looked surprised before he said:

"It sounds as though you have had a very extensive education."

"I like to think so," Ina replied. "The trouble is Papa moved so often that by the time I had found myself teachers and settled down to learn all they could teach me, we were off again!"

"That was just like Roland," Lord Wymonde remarked. "He was always restless, always looking out for something new."

For the first time he thought he could see something of his brother, of whom he had been very fond when they were young, in Ina.

Looking back, he could remember how it was always Roland who had thought up new interests for them both, new adventures in which to take part, and of course new pranks for which they were often severely punished.

It was Roland who had made things exciting, and Lord Wymonde realised now that when he had married and Roland had gone away to live abroad he had taken with him a joy of living which no one else had been able to replace.

"You must tell me about your life with your father," he said aloud.

"It will take a long time," Ina warned. "We did so many things, we went to so many places. It was always such fun and I miss him . . . terribly!"

There was just a little tremor in her voice which Lord Wymonde noticed, and he wondered if his son would ever speak of him like that. He had a feeling he was failing Rupert in a way that it was difficult to formulate.

"Do you live in a very large house?" Ina asked.

"It is certainly large for a London house," Lord Wymonde replied. "Your father used to laugh at it and say it was dark and stuffy, and he much preferred living in the country."

"He has told me so much about Wymonde Park,"

Ina said. "He loved it, and I think it was the one thing he missed really terribly when he lived abroad."

"Then why did he not come home?" Lord Wymonde asked.

Ina considered this for a moment. Then she said:

"I think for one reason because as you were married he would not have been able to live in the big house, and secondly, as I expect you know, Papa was bored by Society."

She gave one of her entrancing little laughs.

"The parties he went to were very different from the ones he described to me as taking place in my grandfather's time."

Lord Wymonde was listening intently.

Now he thought he understood why immediately he married Lucy, Roland had gone abroad for a year, then returned unexpectedly.

For six months he had drifted about London, having a series of love-affairs which were obviously of no particular importance, then he had vanished again.

Lord Wymonde remembered thinking that he was too young to be throwing up the traditional way of living of his class for a life that was obviously Bohemian and as such would be censured and frowned upon.

Yet he knew there was no point in arguing with Roland once he had made up his mind, and although Lord Wymonde had remonstrated with him whenever they met, Roland had gone off for longer and longer periods of time until finally eighteen years ago, after Ina had been born, England saw him no more.

Lord Wymonde remembered going to Italy to tell his brother about their mother's death and to convey the messages she had insisted he should give to his younger brother.

He found Roland in a very attractive Studio with every possible comfort, but which was situated in a part of Rome that fashionable people would not have thought of visiting.

Lord Wymonde had first been appalled by the narrow streets that surrounded it, with its noisy half-naked children, and large-breasted mothers sitting on door-steps unashamedly feeding their babies.

If the place was picturesque, he thought, it certainly smelt and when he entered the house where he had learnt his brother lived, he was determined to persuade him to return to England.

Alternatively to find a more savoury neighbourhood in which to live when he was in Rome.

Then inside the house which was unexpectedly comfortable he had found what he had not expected, that his brother was supremely happy.

When he had been announced it had been just like old times to hear Roland say without any preliminaries:

"Come and look at this, George! Have you ever seen anything so fantastic? Or indeed so beautiful?"

The rather pompous words of greeting George had been about to utter died on his lips as his brother, taking him by the arm, drew him across the room to where on a throne was, Lord Wymonde realised, a model.

She was a child of about ten, an Italian, but with Moorish blood in her. Her jet black hair fell over her naked shoulders while the rags she wore only half-covered her body.

Surrounding her were flowers of every colour which she had obviously been selling when Roland had seen her and had brought not only her wares, but herself into the Studio so that he could paint them.

"Look at the colour of her skin against those camelias!" he exclaimed. "It is fantastic, but God knows if I can get it all down on canvas."

The enthusiasm and excitement in his voice made Lord Wymonde feel as if he too was trying to capture a beauty that was so vivid, and yet so elusive that somehow it would escape him if he did not hurry.

It was a feeling Roland always engendered in him and it was with him all the time he stayed in Rome.

When he went home, leaving Roland, his wife, and his baby behind, he knew he was losing something that was very precious and meant a great deal to him.

He was sensible enough to realise that while Roland was painting he and his family would not fit into an English background or the life that Lord Wymonde was living with Lucy.

After that he only heard from his brother occasionally and it was usually his wife Louise who wrote to thank him for the presents at Christmas, or the good wishes on her husband's birthday.

As the years passed Lord Wymonde had almost forgotten how much Roland meant to him until he died.

Then he felt a sense of loss that made him morose and depressed for several weeks.

He thought when he first received the news that he should go out to Nice where his brother had died and attend the Funeral.

It was Lucy who had pointed out to him sharply and in an extremely practical manner that the Funeral must have been over before the letter announcing Roland's death arrived.

What was more, to cancel all his engagements merely to put a few flowers on his brother's grave would be a quite ridiculous gesture.

"Besides," she added practically, "how do you know the child is still there? There must be somebody looking after her, and they may have taken her away from the empty Villa to somewhere else in France."

When Lord Wymonde had seemed unconvinced by her arguments she had said forcefully:

"Oh, for goodness sake, George! You know how wild and impractical your brother always was. Write to your niece and see if she wants your help, but do not go tearing off on a wild-goose chase. There is no point in it."

She had been so insistent that finally Lord Wymonde had given in and had written to Ina to learn that she was staying for the time being with a Mrs. Harvester and there was, as Lucy had said, no point in his making the long journey to Nice.

At the same time he had the inescapable feeling that he had missed something.

"Why did your father die when he was so young?" he asked Ina now.

"I think he had strained his heart when he and Mama went climbing mountains in Turkey. I was very young at the time, and they left me with some friends while they went off exploring."

"Why Turkey?" Lord Wymonde enquired.

"Where they went was very beautiful, as I saw later from Papa's pictures," Ina replied. "Apparently Papa wanted to sketch a view from the top of a mountain and they were marooned there all night in a storm. After that, sometimes in the winter he would get a very bad cough and complained that his chest hurt him."

Ina made a little gesture with her hands.

"It is the only explanation I can think of as to why his heart was weak, but we never knew how bad it was until he . . . died."

Again there was a note in her voice which made Lord Wymonde know that it hurt her to speak of her father.

Because he wanted her to be happy he said:

"When we go to Wymonde Park I will show you all the places where your father and I played together when we were boys—our house in a tree, the boat on the lake, and our own special sanctum in one of the turrets where nobody else was ever allowed to enter."

"I should love to see them," Ina said. "Papa used to tell me about the hut in the woods where you once spent the night in a snow-storm."

"Of course, I remember that," Lord Wymonde said, "and a very bad storm it was! They had to dig us out when morning came."

"What fun you had!" Ina said. "I used to wish that I had a brother like you."

"You must meet Rupert," Lord Wymonde answered automatically, then added: "But of course, he is too young for you."

He was thinking as he had thought so often before, that Rupert, because he was an only child, could have none of the fun he had had.

"I would have liked several sons," he said to himself, "and a daughter like Ina."

The carriage was driving up Park Lane and Ina was looking first at the Park on one side, then the large, impressive houses on the other.

Lord Wymonde was just about to tell her the names of their distinguished owners, when he thought there would be no point.

How could a child living in the wilds of nowhere have the slightest idea who the noble Marquess of Londonderry was, or the Earl of Dudley?

Instead he said:

"I think your Aunt Lucy will be at home when we arrive, but Wednesday is a day when she entertains."

"Every Wednesday?" Ina asked with interest.

"Most ladies in Society have one day a week when they are at home to their friends at tea time," Lord Wymonde explained. "As it happens, your aunt is so popular that people call on her almost every day. But Wednesday is a fixture."

He was thinking as he spoke that what it really

meant was that on Wednesdays the house would be crowded, while on the other days of the week Lucy's favourites, who were usually of the opposite sex, would drop in, in the hope of finding her alone.

Lord Wymonde was well aware that husbands were expected to make themselves scarce at tea time, which was when he and his contemporaries met at the Club for a game of Bridge, or merely to gossip.

They would sit drinking and talking in the large leather chairs in White's, Boodles, or St. James's, well aware that they should not go home until it was time for them to dress for dinner.

Because he was thinking that it might be nicer for Ina not to be pitch-forked into a room full of strangers, he said as the carriage began to draw up outside Wymonde House:

"I expect you would like to go first to your own bedroom and change before you meet your aunt."

He thought Ina looked rather surprised as she answered:

"Yes, of course, Uncle George, and thank you for thinking of it. But I shall have to wait for Hannah and give her a chance to unpack."

"I tell you what we will do," Lord Wymonde said, "we will go into the Study and while Hannah is unpacking we will see if we can find some sketch books which belonged to your father. I know they are somewhere on the bookshelves."

"I would love to do that," Ina said with a sincerity that was unmistakable, "and I have brought you as a present, Uncle George, two of Papa's smaller pictures. The rest I have stored together with my furniture."

"It was very kind of you to think of me, Ina."

She smiled at him, and he felt as if it warmed his heart.

"I like the child," he told himself, "and I hope we can make her happy."

At the same time he knew that Lucy was going to be difficult.

As her guests, and there had been, Lucy thought, a larger number of them than usual, made their farewells, she found herself wondering for the first time, what had happened to George and his niece.

He had gone off at about three-thirty to the station to meet her, after moving restlessly about the Drawing-Room until Lucy felt it was difficult not to scream at him.

"For goodness sake, George," she said sharply at length, "sit down and stop looking like an agitated hen!"

Her husband did not answer, and after a moment she went on:

"You are working yourself up into a state of fever just because a girl of eighteen is coming to stay with us, and Heaven knows, while it is inconvenient enough for me, there is no reason why it should affect you in any way."

"We have to do our best for Roland's daughter," Lord Wymonde said.

"And we are doing it," Lucy said bitterly. "But *I* have to buy her clothes, *I* have to instruct her how to behave, and *I* have to introduce her to a world of which she is completely and abysmally ignorant."

She gave a spiteful little laugh as she added:

"She very likely eats peas off her knife, and talks with a foreign accent."

Lord Wymonde had been angry.

"There is no need for you to talk like that, Lucy," he said sharply. "You may have disliked my brother, but nobody could say he was not a gentleman, and his wife, who I may say was a very sweet person, came from a distinguished family, so whatever else my niece may be, she will definitely be a lady!"

"I am not questioning her birth, but her manners!" Lucy snapped. "As you are well aware, George, her father was always hob-nobbing either with Hottentots, or whatever those tribes in Africa are called, or with the inhabitants of some Mediterranean slum he thought picturesque."

Lord Wymonde remembered uncomfortably the people he had seen in the streets outside Roland's home in Rome.

He also remembered the loveliness of Louise, and the delicious meals which he had eaten while he had been their guest.

Granted it was not the sort of food that Lucy would have enjoyed, but their Italian cook, who was dressed in a very strange manner and had to his mind been over-familiar, was better than any Chef he could employ in England.

"If your niece disgraces herself at Chale, do not

blame me!" Lucy was saying. "I still think we would be wise to send her to your Cousin Dorothy, who I am quite certain would be only too willing to have her."

"Dorothy is not in London."

Lord Wymonde spoke with a resigned patience, having already turned down the same suggestion a dozen times.

"Well, there must be somebody, whether they are in London or in the country, who would take the girl off our hands," Lucy said. "Heaven knows, there are enough Mondes about when we do not want to see them!"

Lord Wymonde walked to the window.

"I will not argue over this any further, Lucy," he said firmly. "I am tired of this whole subject. I intend to have Ina with us whatever you may say, and I have no intention of changing my plans."

As he finished speaking he walked from the room, slamming the door behind him.

Lucy jumped at the noise, and told herself it was foolish to annoy George.

She knew that once he had made up his mind nothing would change it, and what was far more important was for him not to make a fuss about the Marquis.

"If I am nice to the girl," she reasoned, "he will be so pleased with me that he will forget his suspicions that Irvine means more to me than any other man has ever done before."

The mere thought of the Marquis made her draw in her breath and she knew she was counting the hours until she would see him again.

"I will be charming to George and to his tiresome niece," she decided. "I will find her clothes of some sort, and try to pretend I want to drag her around after me, while, if I am honest, I could murder her with my bare hands!"

Almost instinctively Lucy's eyes went to the mirror over the mantelpiece where she could see herself reflected.

There was no doubt she was looking beautiful.

Her new gown which was of sapphire-blue silk made her skin seem dazzlingly white and appeared to be reflected in her eyes.

There was no one, no one in the whole of London, who had hair that was naturally that vivid gold that men described as coming from the heart of the sun.

Lucy hoped the Marquis would say something like that to her.

He had not yet paid her a compliment, but at least he wanted to kiss her.

She knew that from the way he looked at her and the manner in which his eyes lingered on her mouth.

She felt a little thrill run through her and felt sure that when they were at Chale there would be some opportunity for them to meet alone, and he would kiss her again.

Then she saw her eyes reflected in the mirror were shining and there was a smile on her lips, her first guest had been announced.

Lucy realised now it was after six o'clock and there had been no sign of George or his niece.

Perhaps the train was late; perhaps, if she was very lucky, the girl had fallen into the Channel and been drowned.

But that was too much to hope.

Then a sudden thought struck her. Supposing, just supposing the girl looked so dreadful, so appallingly gauche and ugly, that George had been ashamed to bring her to the Drawing-Room while her guests were there?

Lucy's lips tightened.

If that was true, then nothing would make her take Ina to Chale, or chaperon her.

How could she, who was the epitome of everything that was beautiful, the loveliest woman in England, walk about accompanied by some oafish girl?

What was more, it would be impossible to get her married off, and then if George still had this ridiculous loyalty to his dead brother she would be round their necks like a mill-stone—or was it an albatross? Lucy was very vague about anything to do with Literature.

Two footmen came into the Drawing-Room to remove the tea things.

"Has His Lordship returned?" Lucy asked sharply.

"Yes, M'Lady."

"Where is he?"

"In the Study, M'Lady."

"Alone?"

"He has the young lady with him, M'Lady."

That was all Lucy wanted to know. With a last glance at herself in the mirror she walked from the Drawing-Room and down the stairs to the Hall.

George's ancestors watched her progress from the walls. Ensconced in their gold frames they were on the whole, Lucy had always thought, an unprepossessing lot.

Yet George had been outstandingly good-looking when she first met him, and so had his brother, though Roland had made it very clear that he did not admire her.

That was really why Lucy had never liked him.

George had talked so much about his brother, and people had told her they were alike, so when Lucy met him she expected Roland to be bowled over by her beauty, as his brother had been.

But Roland had looked at her critically and she had known without his telling her that, incredible though it seemed, she not only did not attract him, but he did not even admire her.

It seemed so inconceivable that she had actually said to him:

"I am sure you will want to paint me, as a wedding-present for George. I know it is what he would like."

She was certain that Roland would not only be delighted at the idea but extremely grateful to her for saying that she would sit for him.

After all, he was unknown as an artist, and the family referred to his painting almost as if it was something slightly disreputable, and not exactly what a gentleman should do.

To Lucy's astonishment however Roland had merely said:

"No, thank you!"

"What do you mean—no thank you?"

"I do not wish to paint you."

She was so surprised that she asked him right out why not.

"Because you are too obvious," he replied, "too

predictable and not my idea of beauty. What I want to paint is real beauty."

She had been too humiliated to say any more, but she had never forgiven him and if she was honest, she had hated him from that moment.

When George had come back from Rome after their mother's death he had said:

"Roland's pictures astonish me! They are not the conventional type of paintings that please the Academicians, but they are good, very good indeed!"

"How do you know?" Lucy asked. "You are not a judge of art, George."

"I am quite prepared to admit that," he had answered, "but I met a number of people in Rome whose opinions I respect, and they said things about Roland's pictures which made me very proud."

"I hope you are also proud of the kind of life he leads!" Lucy snapped.

Roland did nothing about his pictures, neither exhibiting them, nor apparently selling them, but friends who met him abroad talked about him as if he had a definite talent.

"If you ask me," Lucy said to George on one occasion when they were discussing Roland, "your brother is frittering away his life, just wasting it!"

"I do not see why you should say that," Lord Wymonde replied. "At least he is creating something."

Lucy had made a derisive sound that apparently angered him, for he added:

"Roland has created a number of pictures while I have only created one son. I think when it is totalled up, he has the advantage of me."

He had left the room before Lucy could find an answer, and she had taken care after that not to bandy words with George about his brother.

'It will serve him right,' she thought spitefully as she neared the Study, 'if Roland's daughter is a monster!'

As she put out her hand towards the door she heard George's voice, then someone laugh.

It was a distinctly musical sound, very young and very natural.

Lucy opened the door.

George was sitting in his favourite chair and on the floor in front of him was a child with fair hair who was turning over a number of sketches one after another.

"Do look at this one, Uncle George," she said. "It is so funny!"

She was laughing again, then the sound died away as she saw Lucy standing in the doorway staring at her.

For a moment there was silence, then Lord Wymonde remembered:

"Ah, there you are, Lucy! This is Ina! We were looking at some sketches her father did when he was a boy."

"I was expecting you upstairs," Lucy said automatically.

She closed the door and came across the room as Ina rose to her feet.

"Can she really be so small, so young, so very— young?" Lucy asked herself.

The word seemed to pierce her like a dagger.

That baby face, pale blue eyes, hair so fine that it looked like silk!

"Is this Ina?" she asked, feeling there must be some mistake.

Ina curtsied.

"How do you do, Aunt Lucy! I am Ina, and I am afraid I am very small."

"You are indeed!" Lucy replied. "And I do not suppose that even heels to your slippers would make very much difference."

She was thinking as she spoke that none of her clothes would even begin to be suitable.

The gown Ina was wearing was surprisingly well made, Lucy thought, and almost passable.

"We did not come upstairs," George was saying a trifle uncomfortably, "because I thought you would rather meet Ina when she was alone, and it would have been embarrassing for her to meet you when you were surrounded by so many strangers."

"I quite understand," Lucy answered in a voice which told her husband she did nothing of the sort.

"But now," she went on, "as time is very short, and doubtless you have explained to Ina where we are going in two days time, I think she should come upstairs and show me what clothes she has with her, before we try frantically to find her something suitable to wear."

"Yes, of course, my dear," George agreed. "As it happens I have not told Ina about going to Chale. You can do that."

He paused as if he suddenly remembered he was not particularly pleased about the idea and added:

"I am sure it is something you are longing to do anyway."

For the moment husband and wife looked in a hostile manner at each other across Ina's head.

But she was down on her knees picking up her father's sketches, and putting them tidily back in the leather folder from which she had taken them.

"Come along, Ina," Lucy said. "You and I have a great deal to do and very little time in which to do it."

Ina put the folder down on the table.

"Thank you very much, Uncle George," she said. "I have loved seeing those sketches, and perhaps we could look at the rest of them another time?"

"We will do that," Lord Wymonde answered.

He smiled at his niece, and she smiled back, but she was aware that Lucy had already left the Study and ran quickly after her.

As they walked up the stairs side by side Lucy said:

"What your uncle omitted to tell you was that you are a very lucky girl in that we are going to stay, on Friday, at one of the most famous and beautiful houses in England."

"I hoped we would be going to Wymonde Park," Ina said without thinking.

"We are here in London for the next two months," Lucy said crossly, "and do not try to inveigle your uncle into taking you there until the Season is over!"

Ina's eyes widened.

She was quick enough to understand that her aunt

did not like Wymonde Park and she understood now why there had been almost a note of longing in Uncle George's voice when he had spoken of it.

She knew too well how much her father would have hated having to be in London when he could have been in the country.

He would want to swim in the lake as he had told her he and his brother had always done several times a day and they had ridden their horses across the Park and hunted in the woods.

"We are going to Chale," Lucy was saying, "and Chale belongs to the Marquis of the same name, who will be your host."

Because she was afraid the way she spoke was too revealing, she added hastily:

"His mother, the Dowager Marchioness, because he is not married, will be your hostess, and there will be a party of extremely interesting and distinguished people, besides your uncle and me—and now you!"

There was no need for her to tell Ina she was not wanted—she had heard it all too clearly in her aunt's voice.

"Perhaps," she said hesitatingly, "you . . . would rather I did not . . . come with you?"

"Your uncle insists that you do so, and I had hoped you would be grateful for an opportunity which does not occur to most girls of your age. Invitations to Chale are, I assure you, prized."

"I . . . I am very honoured," Ina said.

"And so you should be," Lucy replied. "You will understand, I am sure, that it is most important from my point of view, and of course your uncle's, that you should make a good impression and not upset or disgrace us in any way."

She spoke without thinking, and when she saw the expression on Ina's face, she felt slightly discomfited.

"Why should you think I would do that?" Ina enquired.

Lucy realised that she should somehow make amends in case the child should take umbrage and complain to George.

"It is understandable as you have been abroad for so long," she said in a different tone of voice, "that you will find English manners and all the little conventions which are so important in the best circles difficult to remember, even if you knew them in the first place."

Her voice became more patronising as she added:

"You must ask me about anything you do not understand, and of course when you do not know what to do. But first we must look at your clothes."

As Lucy spoke they reached Ina's bedroom.

She had already washed and changed into another gown as soon as Hannah had arrived, and unpacked them for her.

What she had on was the first gown that came out of her trunk, but now Hannah and the housemaid who was helping her, had filled the wardrobe with a number of pretty dresses that Mrs. Harvester had insisted Ina should buy from the very best dressmakers in Nice.

"You cannot wear black in this climate," she had said soon after Ina had gone to live with her. "It is a colour I detest on the very young; it is only for old ladies like me."

"Papa always said mourning was a barbaric custom," Ina said.

"I agree with your father, and therefore I want you to choose the colours that will suit you," Mrs. Harvester said. "I like beautiful things around me."

"You have beautiful things!" Ina cried. "I have never seen such exquisite furniture or such glorious pictures!"

She paused, then as if she felt she was being disloyal, she added:

"I love Papa's pictures because they are so alive and they seem to glow with colour and vitality, but yours are beautiful in a very different way, and I love them too."

She had been staring as she spoke, at an exquisite Guardi, thinking no one could portray more perfectly the Venice that had entranced her when they had lived there for a brief time, two years ago.

Mrs. Harvester had been very critical about what Ina should and should not wear.

"Because you are so small," she had said, "you must have gowns that will not only flatter your personality, but also suit your height. Never be slavish to fashion, Ina. It is an easy path for the lazy and for those without any taste of their own."

Ina had laughed at the way Mrs. Harvester had spoken, although she knew she was serious.

The dressmakers had brought sketches and materials to the Villa, and Ina would stand almost as if she was one of her father's models for hours on end, until Mrs. Harvester was satisfied that the gown that was being designed and made for her, was exactly right.

Sometimes to Ina's consternation when the gown was actually finished Mrs. Harvester would not let her wear it.

"What is wrong with it?"

"It is too old for you," she would say. "You must throw it away, or give it to the poor."

At other times she would be delighted because Ina looked exactly as she wanted her to look.

Ina had said to Hannah:

"In her own way Mrs. Harvester is an artist just as Papa was."

She knew Hannah did not understand, and explained:

"She wants to portray beauty on me, just as Papa wanted to portray it on canvas. I do wish he had known her better."

"Your father liked being with young people," Hannah said almost as if she spoke to herself.

"I think that is because he felt young himself," Ina replied. "Old people never seem to get excited about things as Papa did."

But Mrs. Harvester quietly and without saying very much had, Ina felt, been excited about her gowns.

It had given her a new interest, just as having Ina and Hannah to stay had. Instead of sitting alone day after day in the garden or the Villa, she would take Ina on drives around the countryside and occasionally they went in a boat out on the sea.

It was all rather slow, so different from the speed with which they were always doing something new when her father had been alive.

At the same time as she had so many other interests with her teachers, Ina had been happy.

Now, as she watched her aunt only too ready to criticize her gowns Ina felt, and find fault, she wondered exactly what her new life in England would be like.

"I must admit your clothes are better than I had expected," Lucy remarked grudgingly, as Hannah held up Ina's gowns one by one, for her inspection.

"They're French, M'Lady," Hannah replied, "and we always believed when we were living in France, that the French were one step in front of the English when it came to clothes, if nothing else."

"I am well aware of that!" Lucy said crushingly.

Hannah realised she had presumed upon her place and retreated into what Ina called "her shell."

"I am afraid I did not introduce Hannah to you properly, Aunt Lucy," Ina said quickly. "She has looked after me ever since I was born, and Papa and Mama relied on her for everything."

She paused and glanced at Lucy anxiously, thinking there was an uninterested expression on her face.

"When Papa died I should have been lost if Hannah had not been there," she added.

"I am sure you have done your duty," Lucy said to Hannah, but the words did not sound like a compliment.

"I did my best, M'Lady."

Hannah was astute enough to realise that she had made a mistake, and that in defending her Ina had made things worse rather than better.

Lucy turned towards the door.

"I shall have to take you shopping tomorrow, Ina, as I see there are many extra things you require," she said. "But it is obvious to me that owing to your size it will be completely impossible to find you anything new to wear at Chale. You will just have to make do with what you have."

She left the room before Ina could reply.

Then as the door closed behind her she ran towards Hannah and put her arms around her.

"Thank goodness you are here, Hannah, dearest!" she said. "I know now why Papa had no wish to see his relations, although I sometimes felt he missed his brother."

"Now Miss Ina," Hannah admonished, "don't you go making hasty judgements when there's no need for them. It'll all seem strange at first, you knew that. But this is where you belong."

Ina kissed Hannah on the cheek.

"If it is too difficult and Aunt Lucy makes it clearer than she has already, that she does not want me, we can always go back to Nice. We have nearly a houseful of furniture there already."

"We'll do nothing of the sort, Miss Ina!" Hannah said sharply. "When you know England better you'll love it, and quite frankly, I'm glad for one to be back with civilised people again. I never did have much time for all them foreigners!"

Ina gave a laugh and it swept away the worry from her eyes.

"I know exactly why you are glad to be back, Hannah," she said. "It is all that gossip over the tea cups that you have missed. The French, the Spanish, and the Italians could never do that properly, could they?"

"They could not!" Hannah agreed stoutly. "But

you'll be properly late for dinner, Miss Ina, if you don't start undressing while I get your bath ready. They have their meals on time in England, and don't you forget it."

"Tomorrow I will buy myself a reliable watch," Ina promised.

But she was laughing as she started to undo her gown.

Chapter Three

INA WENT down to dinner behind Lucy thinking that she was taking part in a wonderful and exciting play.

Although she expected something magnificent after all that had been said about Chale, it certainly exceeded her expectations, and as they drove down the drive she could hardly breathe in case it was a mirage that would vanish in front of her eyes.

As the train bringing them from London was late, there was only time when they arrived to be greeted by the Major Domo and a very awe-inspiring housekeeper who took them to their bedrooms.

Ina knew that Lucy was flattered when the housekeeper said:

"We've given Your Ladyship your favourite rooms in the West Wing."

"Thank you," Lucy replied, a little purring note in her voice that Ina had begun to recognise.

The rooms in the West Wing were certainly impressive. There was a *Boudoir* that was filled with malmaison carnations which Ina guessed, because there were vases of them in London, were her aunt's favourite flower.

Then there was a magnificent bedroom with a painted veiling of rioting gods and cupids, and opening out of it first a dressing-room for Lord Wymonde, and beyond that another extremely attractive room for Ina.

"His Grace thought, M'Lady, that as she was new to Chale the young lady would wish to be close to Your Ladyship," the housekeeper said.

"How kind," Lucy murmured.

But Ina thought there was something false in the way she spoke and was quite certain that her aunt would not want her to be near enough to worry her or ask a lot of questions.

Then Hannah appeared and started to unpack her clothes, some of which were just as they had been brought from Nice, and she began to tut-tut over the fact that they had naturally become somewhat creased after the journey.

"Don't worry, Miss Hannah," the housemaid said, "when there's a house-party we always have two maids permanently in the ironingroom who can press anything wanted at any time."

Ina thought with amusement that Hannah was going to enjoy Chale.

Before she had come to her mother to look after her when she was a baby, Hannah had been employed in a very grand house as under-nursery-maid to the children of the Duke.

When she was small Ina used to be fascinated by Hannah's stories of the Ducal children, and more especially of the protocol that took place in the household itself.

As she grew older, she realised that the servants are far more class-conscious than their masters and mistresses, and she knew now that Hannah would be very conscious of her status in the housekeeper's room.

It was a good thing from her point of view that Uncle George had a title.

'Perhaps she will be able to sit at meals on the right-hand side of the Butler,' Ina thought.

She knew that was the place of honour for any visiting maid, but naturally it depended on whether the other ladies staying in the house were of greater social distinction.

She walked round the room while Hannah and the housemaid were unpacking, looking at the writing table where there were dozens of little items that were apparently required if one was to write a letter.

But she was far more interested in a table near the bed on which were arranged half-a-dozen books.

It had always been difficult in France to obtain enough books to read, even though Mrs. Harvester belonged to the best Library in Nice, which on her instructions faithfully sent to England for what was required.

She bought French books galore, but because her

father was no longer with her Ina wanted to read more about the country to which she belonged and to which, because he was dead, she had the anxious feeling she would have to return.

The history books were disappointing.

She found she could learn more from novels, and she read through Jane Austen and the Brontës, interested in the stories, but even more intrigued by the descriptions of English life that the books portrayed.

She was deep in one of the novels she had found in her bedroom when Hannah told her that time was getting on and her bath was ready.

It had been brought into the room from the cupboard where it was kept outside and placed on a large bath-mat embroidered with the Marquis's coronet on the hearth-rug.

In the winter, Ina thought, it would be delightful to bathe in front of a roaring fire, but the present weather was too warm for that and she thought she was unlikely to want both of the large brass cans of steaming hot water which had been carried into the room by two housemaids.

She already knew from Hannah that a footman would bring the cans of water upstairs and put them outside the door, and the housemaids then carried them in, finding them extremely heavy when they were full.

It seemed to involve much labour, and she thought how much easier it had been when her father had a house by the sea to run over the sands and into the waves, then to feel tinglingly fresh when the water was cold.

Hannah had already warned her not to say too

much when she was in England about bathing in the sea.

"Why not?" Ina asked.

"Because English ladies don't appear in public unless they're fully dressed."

Ina had laughed.

"There was no one to see Papa and me on that beach in Africa, or when we were in Greece two summers ago."

"It's still not the sort of thing a lady does," Hannah said primly.

"Poor ladies!" Ina exclaimed. "They obviously have a miserable time."

She knew however, that Hannah was being wise in warning her not to say anything which people like Aunt Lucy would think was wrong, and which would reflect not only on her but on her father.

She was quite certain from what he had told her that if his relations disapproved of him, as he always said they did, they would be ready to disapprove of her.

"I must be careful," Ina told herself.

After what Aunt Lucy had said on her arrival, she was sure that they were expecting her to behave in an outlandish manner.

When she was dressed for dinner she knew that the white gown with a small bustle at the back, surmounted with a bow of ribbon that was part of the sash, was in perfect good taste, although its very simplicity was deceptive.

It had been an expensive gown, and Mrs. Harvester had approved of it because as she had said, it made Ina look like a lily.

"Lilies have such a beautiful line," she said approvingly. "Their petals are never over-decorated, and that is the perfection you must aim for, dear child, in your dress."

"I am listening to everything you tell me," Ina said with a smile.

She knew that just as her father drew the right lines in his sketches, so Mrs. Harvester looked for the line which made a gown either smart or dowdy.

She had arranged her hair very simply, with just a few curls at the back of her head, and when Lord Wymonde saw her he thought it would be hard for any young girl to look lovelier or more exactly as she should, when she was stepping out into the grown-up world for the first time.

He had knocked on Ina's door to ask her if she was ready, and when he entered she ran to him and slipped her hand into his.

"It is very exciting to be here with you, Uncle George," she said, "and in such a magnificent house that I think even Papa would have been impressed."

"I would like to think so," Lord Wymonde replied, "but I have a feeling that he would be laughing at all the pomp and circumstance and wanting to go off on his own to camp out in a tent in the park."

Ina laughed.

"He might have done that when he was young, but when he grew older he rather appreciated the comfort of a soft bed."

She was laughing when from the open door which led from Lord Wymonde's dressing-room into Lucy's room, a voice said coldly:

"What is going on? I am waiting, George, for you to escort me downstairs!"

"I was just collecting Ina, my dear," Lord Wymonde replied.

"I am not waiting for anyone!" Lucy said.

A maid opened the door into the passage and she stepped out looking, Ina thought as she followed her, as beautiful as the goddesses on the painted ceilings, or the marble statues which graced the huge Hall.

They walked in silence until they reached the large double doors where two footmen in powdered wigs were waiting to open them.

Because it was an intimate house-party of friends they were not announced, and as Lucy sailed into the room the Marchioness gave a cry of delight, and went towards her, both hands outstretched.

Ina thought it would have been impossible for her to wear any more diamonds without their overlapping.

"I am so delighted to see you, dearest Lucy," the Marchioness was saying, "and you, dear George! I know Irvine has some new horses which he wants you to admire."

"I am content for the moment to admire you, Alice," Lord Wymonde said a little ponderously. "And this is Roland's daughter."

The Marchioness turned her attention to Ina who had been looking at her with sparkling eyes, fascinated by her appearance and the quick, gushing manner in which she spoke.

Hastily she curtsied.

"I remember your father well," the Marchioness

66

said. "He was an extremely handsome man, and danced divinely, when we could persuade him to do so."

She did not wait for Ina to reply, but led them towards the rest of the party who were congregated on the other side of the room.

It was then that Ina realised that her Aunt Lucy was talking to the most handsome man she had ever seen.

He was tall, broad-shouldered and his dark hair was swept back from his square-cut forehead. She knew without being told that this was the Marquis of Chale, and her host.

He was saying something to her aunt that she could not hear.

Then he held out his hand to her Uncle George, saying:

"It is delightful to see you, George. I know my mother has already told you that I have just bought half-a-dozen horses of which I hope you will approve."

"I am certainly only too ready to try them out," Lord Wymonde answered.

The Marquis looked towards Ina and as Lucy was silent, Lord Wymonde said:

"This is my niece, Ina. She has only just arrived here from France, and we are grateful that we could bring her with us."

"There is always room at Chale for any of your relations," the Marquis smiled.

He held out his hand and Ina gave him hers.

As he touched her she felt a vibration from his fingers and told herself that she liked him.

Her father had said to her:

"You can tell a man's character by his handshake. Avoid the flabby sort, or the aggressive type who squeeze your fingers, and especially those who are so damned condescending that they behave as if they are giving you a present."

"What are the right sort?"

"You will know that when you touch a person," her father answered.

Ina had been quite small when he told her this, but because it amused her, she would try to guess people's characters by the way they shook hands.

As she grew older she found that her first impression was always right and she could never remember making a mistake.

"As I gather this is your first house-party," the Marquis was saying, "I hope we can make it enjoyable for you."

"I am enjoying it already!" Ina replied, "and your house is so wonderful that I find I have no words with which to describe it."

It was obvious from the rapture in her voice that she was sincere, and the Marquis smiled.

Then Lucy said insistently:

"Tell me what amusements you have arranged for us tomorrow."

"They are to be a surprise," the Marquis answered.

Ina longed to know what the surprise was, but her uncle was drawing her away to introduce her to other members of the party.

There was an attractive woman who said some very pleasant things to her and Ina gathered her name was Mrs. Marshall.

There were several other ladies who looked at her, she thought, with surprise. Then her uncle was introducing her to the men.

They looked very elegant in their stiff white shirts and high collars, and they all, Ina noticed, seemed to have something to say to her uncle about horses and the races which she gathered they had attended the previous week.

Then one man came up and said in a somewhat autocratic tone:

"Good-evening, Wymonde! I hope you will introduce me to your niece. She looks like the first snow-drop of spring."

"Good-evening, Your Highness!" Lord Wymonde replied. "This is my brother's daughter, Ina. You may remember Roland."

"I last saw him some years ago in Cairo," was the reply, "but he said he did not like the place and was leaving the next day."

Ina gave a little laugh. It sounded so like her father.

"This, Ina," her uncle said, "is Prince Ivan Romanouski. I do not know if you are old enough to remember your father's visit to Egypt?"

"Of course I remember it," Ina answered. "I think I was ten at the time. Papa was really annoyed because a camel stood on two of his canvases and ate his paints!"

"That was certainly a disaster," the Prince said, "and how often did your father paint you?"

"Not more often than he could help," Ina smiled. "He said I was a very bad model and would never keep still."

"I should have thought no artist could resist you."

She realised while they had been speaking the Prince was still holding her hand.

His grip was firm, and yet as she took her hand away she thought she did not want to touch him again.

There was nothing wrong, it was just that she had the feeling in some way, that he was encroaching upon her.

"We must talk about your time in Egypt," the Prince said, "and I shall be interested to know what other parts of the world you have visited."

"There were a great number of them," Ina said warningly.

"I am prepared to listen, however many there may be."

The way he spoke told her that he might be inclined to be tiresome, as some of the older men had been one winter in Italy when they had kept trying to kiss her and asking her to sit on their knee.

"Leave the child alone!" her father had said irritably. "She is too old for that sort of thing!"

There was one quite elderly man who insisted on bringing her presents and wanting her to be grateful for them, until her father had said in his usual impetuous manner:

"I have had enough of this place! We will go to Nice."

Ina had been glad they were to leave entirely because she was tired of saying "No" to the elderly man.

She hoped now that the Prince, although it was very unlikely, would not behave in the same way.

Yet she was glad when her uncle introduced her

to another man who merely said something kind and started to talk about horses.

"It is just a small, cosy party tonight," Ina heard the Marchioness say. "Tomorrow there will be a band, and all the amusing people in the County will be coming to dinner. But I always think on Friday everybody is tired and should go to bed early."

Ina wondered why they should be tired considering none of them worked or did anything but enjoy themselves, but she supposed they stayed up late, either dancing or gambling, and that could be quite exhausting.

She was so entranced by the Dining-Room when they reached it that she found it difficult to listen to what anybody was saying.

Never had she seen such magnificence, with murals covering the walls between pillars of pink marble, while the Dining-Room table was, she thought, a poem in itself.

The Marquis sat at one end with Lucy on his right, his mother at the other end with Lord Wymonde on her left and the Prince on her other side.

Ina had hoped she would not be near the Prince, and found to her relief, that she was in the middle of the table with a man called Harry Trevelyn on one side, and on the other a slightly younger man who was deep in conversation, a rather intimate one, with the lady on his other side.

The table was covered with gold ornaments and in the centre was an arrangement of orchids which was very beautiful.

To Ina the whole room looked like a scene from an Opera, or one of the more magnificent spectacles she had seen in the Theatres in Paris.

She was about to say something when she re-membered that Hannah had said when they had been there:

"Your father may take you to the Theatre, but that's not something you could do if you were living in England."

"Why ever not?" Ina enquired.

"Because young ladies are not supposed to see plays unless they are by Shakespeare or someone really respectable."

"I am glad I am not in England and trying to be a young lady," Ina had said.

"I don't suppose it would do you much harm," Hannah said in her uncompromising voice. "At the same time, I don't know what your relatives would say about it."

"Why should they know?" Ina asked. "And if they did, why should they care?"

Now she told herself that was another thing she would have to keep, as her father would have said: 'under her hat.'

"I expect you are impressed with Chale," Mr. Trevelyn said.

"Of course I am!" Ina replied. "It is such a fan-tastic house that I could not even begin to imagine it, if I were not here."

"That is what I thought when I first saw it," he remarked.

"Do you come here often?" Ina enquired.

There was a little pause. Then he replied:

"As a matter of fact, I live here!"

"How lovely for you!"

"Yes, it is, is it not?"

He did not explain and she wondered what his position was in the household.

Then she forgot about him because she was watching the Marquis at the end of the table, thinking he looked almost like a King in his high-backed chair which was upholstered in red velvet.

With a crown on his head, Ina told herself, he would look exactly like one of the Kings she had seen in the history-books.

Then she saw her aunt's ear-rings swinging as she talked to him and felt because she was so beautiful that her aunt should be in a fairy-story too.

"Of course because he is a King that will please him," Ina told herself, and added: "There should be a Princess at the other end of the table instead of his mother, and this would be a Palace in which, because he had found her after a long, laborious search, they would live happily ever afterwards."

She was wondering what the Princess in her story would look like.

As the Marquis was dark, then she should be fair like Aunt Lucy, but of course younger, and he should rescue her, perhaps like Perseus from the sea-dragon, or from a huge eagle that was carrying her away to its nest in the mountains.

She felt because everything about her was so spectacular that it was impossible to think of these people as being ordinary human beings, men and women who could live anywhere else except where they were now, or be upset by such troubles as poverty, hunger and illness.

"Perhaps this is really Mount Olympus," Ina told

herself, "and they are all gods and goddesses."

Without really meaning to, she was watching the Marquis with eyes very wide in her face, and as if her eyes drew his attention to herself she was aware that he was looking at her and for a moment it was almost as if he spoke to her down the length of the table.

Just for a moment there were only his dark eyes and everything else disappeared. Then Lucy attracted his attention and Ina was aware that Mr. Trevelyn was asking her a question for the third time.

After dinner the gentlemen joined the ladies in another Salon even more beautiful than the one in which they had sat before dinner.

There were card-tables arranged at one end, but everybody seemed to prefer to talk.

Because no one was paying any attention to her, Ina moved as she had wanted to do for sometime towards the display-tables set in an alcove on one side of the room.

She was aware because she had seen similar ones in Paris, that they were French, and as she expected they contained snuff-boxes set with diamonds and other precious stones, miniatures in exquisite frames of enamel and pearls, and other small objects of coral, jade and crystal which she knew were old, rare, and very valuable.

She was staring down at them, wishing she could open the case and hold them in her hands, when someone was beside her and she looked up to see the Marquis standing there.

"You are admiring my treasures," he said.

"They are very fine," Ina replied. "Finer than any I have seen anywhere else in the world."

"I understand you have travelled a lot, and that is therefore a compliment," he said.

"You must be used to them," Ina replied, "but I was thinking just now that only a poem could describe this house, and everything in it."

"What poem is that?" the Marquis asked.

"'In Xanadu did Kubla Khan, a stately pleasure dome decree,'" Ina quoted.

He laughed.

"That is indeed a compliment. And you think I look like Kubla Khan? Is that who you were comparing me to, at dinner?"

"No, at dinner I thought you looked like a King," Ina said simply.

"Knowing the difficulties and troubles of most Kings," the Marquis said, "I can say quite sincerely that I am thankful I am not one."

"But your Kingdom would be a fairy-tale one, without any of the more mundane troubles," Ina said, "and certainly no revolutions!"

"In those circumstances," the Marquis laughed, "I am perfectly prepared to accept the crown!"

"On the other hand," she said, "I was just wondering if, after all, this house and the people here might not be a modern Olympus."

"It is certainly an idea," the Marquis agreed, "but I think you will find, if you read Greek mythology, that even the gods had their problems and difficulties, their dramas and tragedies."

"Of course," Ina said, "otherwise there would be nothing to do, and they would soon have been bored, just eating ambrosia and drinking nectar."

It suddenly struck her that actually the expression on the Marquis's face that she had seen at dinner had been one of boredom.

Perhaps that was not quite the right word, but he looked as if everything that was happening was familiar, so while there was no likelihood of any surprise, there was also no spontaneity or excitement.

It was as if suddenly she had solved a problem she had not consciously realised was there, and yet it had been in the back of her mind.

"What are you thinking?" the Marquis asked.

Because she was living in a kind of dreamland, Ina said truthfully:

"I have just discovered, like the wicked fairy at your Christening, what is missing in your life."

"And what is that?" the Marquis asked.

"Excitement!" she said. "The excitement of the unknown and the unexpected."

Even as she finished speaking in the frank manner in which she would have spoken to her father, she was aware that she had made a mistake.

The Marquis was staring at her in a manner that she was not quite certain registered surprise or indignation.

"I am ... sorry ... I did not mean to sound ... critical ..." she began to say hastily, but Lucy was beside them.

"How sweet of you to be kind to little Ina," she said, "but I am hoping you will come and join me at Baccarat. Harry is arranging the table, and we all want to play."

"Of course," the Marquis agreed. "I imagine your niece will not be interested in a game of chance?"

"Not *my* niece," Lucy replied. "George's, and of course she is much too young to gamble."

She slipped her arm through the Marquis's and as she drew him away Ina asked herself how she could have been so stupid as to reveal what was in her thoughts.

"It was rude of me, and what is more the Marquis will think I am half-witted," she said to herself.

She had been carried away by her own fantasy, and she knew that spoken either in French or Italian what she had said would not have seemed so crude.

'I made a mistake,' she thought, 'and although Papa would have laughed, these people would not think it funny.'

Because she felt embarrassed and at the same time some of the excitement she had felt had slipped away from her, she decided to go to bed.

She knew her aunt did not want her and when she looked for her uncle he was near the gaming tables, talking to that nice Mrs. Marshall.

"I will go to bed and read," Ina decided. "To-morrow if I get the chance, I will tell the Marquis I am sorry, but anyway I do not suppose that he will remember what I said."

She walked towards the door and she had almost reached it when a voice asked:

"Where are you going to, pretty lady?"

It was the Prince, and Ina was sure that the look in his eyes was one she had no wish to see.

"I am going to bed, Your Highness," she replied. "Good-night."

He put out his hand towards her and started to say something, but quickly, so quickly that he could not stop her, she had opened the door and slipped through it.

Outside she ran across the marble Hall and started to climb the gilt and crystal staircase.

She had almost reached the top when looking down she saw the Prince come from the direction of the Salon and she was certain he was looking for her.

She did not stop to find out but hurried along the passages to the West Wing and let herself into her bedroom with a sigh of relief.

When Hannah had suggested waiting up for her, Ina had laughed at the idea.

"I have been putting myself to bed for the last ten years," she said, "and you know as well as I do, Hannah, you will be enjoying yourself telling the staff of your travels."

"They won't be interested," Hannah replied. "All they want to talk about is the Prince of Wales. We may have met some strange people, Miss Ina, but we didn't have the acquaintance of the Prince of Wales!"

"I suppose a Sultan or two, and that bandit whom Papa insisted on painting, would not count in the same way?" Ina teased.

"Certainly not!" Hannah retorted, "and if there was a man I wouldn't have trusted with a four-penny piece, it was him!"

"They may have known Princes, perhaps even Queens," Ina said, "but you have done things they would not dare to do, Hannah. Do you remember when we were chased by those thieves in the Sahara desert? And when we got lost in some outlandish place in Albania and had to spend the night in a cave that smelt of wolves?"

"I don't want to remember those things, Miss Ina, but rather when we had a nice cosy little house, easy to run, and we were able to pick our own fruit off the trees without having to buy it."

Ina thought of her mother and gave a little sigh.

"I often think of that fig-tree in Cyprus," she said. "I waited and watched for the figs to ripen, then Papa made us all leave about two weeks before they did."

"You'll be able to eat enough figs in this place without harking back over those you lost," Hannah retorted, "besides peaches, muscat grapes and every fruit you can think of."

"But I will not be allowed to pick them myself," Ina replied.

She was sure now as she saw her nightgown laid on the bed and the lighted candles burning on the dressing-table that Hannah was enjoying herself downstairs, as she had been unable to do for many, many years.

'Hannah will love Chale in her own way, just as I shall,' she thought.

Then she was thinking of the Marquis, and wishing she had not been so stupid in speaking her thoughts.

As it happened, the Marquis later that evening was speaking of her, but not to Lucy.

He was too astute not to realise that Ina would

be a very unpopular topic of conversation as far as her aunt was concerned.

But after the ladies had gone to bed and the gentlemen were having a last night-cap he said to Lord Wymonde:

"Tell me about your niece, George. She is very lovely, if surprisingly very tiny."

"I thought when I first saw her," Lord Wymonde replied, "that it was typical of Roland who spent his life seeking beauty to produce anything so attractive."

The Marquis nodded his agreement and he said:

"She is intelligent, too."

"That is what I think," Lord Wymonde agreed, "but I suppose travelling in such strange places and meeting all sorts of extraordinary characters must have educated her in a different way from the average young woman who leaves the schoolroom knowing nothing except how to get herself a husband!"

"I do not think you will have any difficulty in finding one for your niece," the Marquis remarked.

"That is up to Lucy," Lord Wymonde said, "and as she has no wish to chaperon the girl, I expect she will get her up the aisle as quickly as possible."

Before the Marquis could speak, they were joined by the Prince.

"I heard you talking about that fascinating, attractive child you brought with you," he said to Lord Wymonde.

"She is eighteen," Lord Wymonde remarked.

He did not care for the Prince, although he was extremely popular amongst the ladies. He was very rich, but also something of a mystery.

He spent three-quarters of the year in Europe and returned to Russia for three months to attend to what were quoted as being his "vast estates" there.

To Lord Wymonde the Prince was a man who evaded all responsibility and in his opinion spent far too much time womanizing and making love to other men's wives.

"She is like a jewel, and you will find that there are dozens of men eager to possess her," the Prince was saying.

Lord Wymonde realised with a sense of annoyance that he was still speaking of Ina.

"She is very young," he said quietly, "too young, as it happens, for this sort of party, but there was nowhere else for her to go. I hope Your Highness will not pay her too many compliments. I would not want her head turned before she has seen a little more of the world."

"You may of course be right, George," the Marquis said smiling, "but when she was with her father she saw a very different world, and an experience which I find intriguing."

"It is certainly a world you have never seen," Lord Wymonde agreed.

He was thinking as he spoke of the slums in Rome and the half-Italian, half-Moorish model that his brother had been painting when he had visited him there.

Then he was surprised to hear the Marquis say with an unusual note of seriousness in his voice:

"Perhaps that is something I am missing."

A few minutes later Lord Wymonde went up to bed.

He knew if he lingered any longer Lucy would

accuse him of waking her up when she had got to sleep, and that meant they would be likely to spend several hours of the night squabbling about it.

He decided therefore that he would certainly not wake her if she was asleep, but spend the night in his dressing-room as he had often done before.

When he went quietly into the *Boudoir* he could see there was a light under Lucy's door and he opened it anxiously to find that she was not yet in bed, but sitting in front of the mirror inspecting her face.

It was something he had seen her do too often for it to make him curious.

"Is that you, George?" she asked.

"Yes, dear. I have come up to bed."

"And about time," she said automatically. "I should have been furious if you had wakened me."

"I would not have done that—I would have slept in my dressing-room."

"I think that is a good idea anyway. I want to sleep late tomorrow morning so that I shall look my best for the party in the evening."

"Very well, my dear," Lord Wymonde agreed.

There was a pause as if they were both thinking what to say next. Then Lucy remarked:

"You must remember tomorrow to tell your niece not to try and force herself on the Marquis. I cannot imagine what Alice must have thought of the way she had him cornered this evening in the alcove, instead of letting him look after his guests."

"By that I imagine you mean yourself," Lord Wymonde said.

The way he spoke told Lucy she had been foolish

to attack Ina. She might have guessed that her husband would go to the child's defence.

She had been furious when she had looked round to see that Ina and the Marquis were talking together in the alcove. Not only were they alone but it was quite obvious that the Marquis was interested in what she was saying.

"He was just being kind," Lucy told herself.

At the same time she was once again aware how young Ina looked and, although she would never admit it, extremely attractive in her white gown.

'It was a terrible mistake to bring her here!' Lucy thought.

As she came upstairs she had been trying to think of how she could keep Ina well away from the Marquis.

Because it was uppermost in her mind she now risked provoking George by saying:

"Alice tells me that there are some charming young people coming to dinner tomorrow evening, and I have persuaded her to put your niece next to the most eligible young bachelor in the County. I am sure that will please her and make you happy."

"I want her to enjoy herself," Lord Wymonde said, in an obstinate tone.

"Of course you do, George, and it is so like your warm-hearted, generous nature to worry over a young girl who, from what I have seen of her, is very capable of taking care of herself."

Lord Wymonde with an unusual perception thought that most men looking at Ina would want to protect her and believe, rightly or wrongly, that she was quite helpless without their assistance.

He knew that was the sort of thing he could not say to his wife, and he moved to her side and put his hand on her shoulder.

"Good-night, my dear! Sleep well! I will try not to disturb you when I get up in the morning."

"Thank you, George. You are always so considerate," Lucy replied.

He kissed her cheek, then was aware of the exotic fragrance of her and the softness of her skin.

His fingers tightened and he said in a voice that was a little deeper than it had been before:

"You looked beautiful tonight, my dear. I was very, very proud of you!"

He would have kissed her again, but Lucy moved sharply.

"I am tired, George," she said, "simply dropping with fatigue!"

For a moment Lord Wymonde was still.

Then his hand fell to his side, and he turned and walked across the room, past the large four-poster with its seductive satin curtains and secretive shadows.

He opened the door of the dressing-room and as he did so he looked back.

His wife was once again scrutinising her face in a hand-mirror.

He gave a little sigh and went into the dressing-room.

Chapter Four

THE MARQUIS, riding through the Park on one of his exceptionally fine horses, thought there was nowhere more attractive than England in the spring.

He realised it was not an original thought and a great number of people, including Lord Byron, had said it before him, but it was difficult not to appreciate the daffodils that were a golden carpet under the trees, or the feeling that everything was fresh and young.

It made him think of Ina and of how many people at the Ball last night had said how attractive she was.

It struck him as strange that she should have been singled out when three of the most beautiful and sophisticated older women in London were in the house-party.

Lucy in particular had been looking superb and her tiara of turquoises and diamonds had seemed to echo the blue of her eyes which shone every time the Marquis came near her.

When they danced together he was well aware that she was thrilled because they were so close, and he was flattered that the woman who was privately known as "The Iceberg" amongst his friends in the Club, was obviously excited by him.

It was always supposed that while women were gossips men were silent and discreet, but anyone as beautiful as Lucy was bound to be discussed.

Ever since the Marquis could remember, men when they were talking amongst themselves described her as "beautiful but a glacier."

They usually added something somewhat indiscreet, voicing their preference for more responsive women, and while the Marquis had made no comment it had been impossible for him not to remember what had been said.

Last night when he looked into Lucy's blue eyes he had known that she was his for the taking, and it was only a question of their having the opportunity.

He was however too sensible and too aware of his position as host to dance with Lucy too many times without performing his duty dances.

As he had said, all the most amusing people in the County had been invited: sixty sat down to dinner in the great Dining-Room and an equal number had arrived after dinner from neighbouring houses.

Because the Marquis intended the party to amuse

Lucy there were no girls, although a number of young men had been invited to squire the women who had no wish to dance with their husbands.

But Lucy had seen that Ina had plenty of partners, and she felt that not only would George think she was behaving in exactly the right way, but it also kept Ina from drawing the attention of the Marquis.

He had in fact danced with her very late in the evening, after a number of the guests had already left.

As he expected she was as light as thistle-down, and although it was the early hours of the morning, she was still bubbling over with an irrepressible vitality that he found attractive.

"You have enjoyed yourself?" he asked.

"It has been wonderful!" she exclaimed. "My first Ball in England, and I do wish I could tell Papa about it."

"Do you think he would have been pleased?" the Marquis asked.

He spoke a little cynically, knowing he had heard not only from Lucy, but from a great number of other people how much Roland Monde had disliked Society and everything about it.

Ina had understood what he was saying, and replied:

"Papa would not have enjoyed it himself, but he liked me to have new experiences, whatever they might be, and this is certainly new."

"You sound," the Marquis said, "as if you have been to very different types of dances."

Ina laughed.

"That is true, but I do not think I should tell you about them. You would be shocked."

"I feel that is unlikely," the Marquis replied, "but risk it, and tell me."

Ina hesitated, and as if he knew what she was thinking, he said:

"Anything you say to me is naturally in confidence. I would not repeat it to anyone."

They were both aware of the person who most especially was not to know anything about Ina's past, and the Marquis said simply:

"Please trust me."

Ina smiled at him.

"Very well, but I warn you, the dancers I have seen would not be considered suitable for a young *lady*."

She accentuated the word "lady" in a refined voice which made him laugh and she went on:

"Papa took me to see the Dervishes dance when we were in Algiers."

"That is certainly astonishing!" the Marquis agreed. "I wish I could have seen them myself."

He was well aware that the Dervishes were the most extraordinary, exotic, and fantastic dancers in the whole of Africa.

They were a Muslim fraternity and the dance of the Dervishes induced an hypnotic trance in which they howled, whirled, and even cut themselves with knives without feeling any pain.

The Marquis occasionally met men who had seen such performances but he had never thought it possible for a lady, especially one as young as Ina, to be present.

"We have talked about me being shocked," he said aloud, "but what about you?"

"Papa explained to me a long time ago," Ina

replied, "that usually things are shocking only when they are deliberately coarse, vulgar, and performed against the better instincts of the person who does them."

She looked up at the Marquis to see if he understood and went on:

"The Dervishes are dedicated to their dancing. It is a religion to them and if those watching interpret it in a different way because they have different standards, that is not the fault of the dancers."

The Marquis thought this was an explanation of primitive ceremonies that he had never heard before. Then when he was wanting to ask Ina more, the dance came to an end and Lucy was beside him.

"Ina dear," she said in a honey-sweet voice which always sounded insincere, "His Highness is waiting to have one last good-night dance with you. Then I think you really should go to bed. I cannot have you losing your beauty sleep."

Ina saw the expression in the Prince's eyes and felt she could not bear him to touch her.

"You are right, Aunt Lucy," she said quickly. "It is late, and I am very tired. Perhaps His Highness will forgive me if I do not dance any more."

She saw the Prince was about to protest and before Lucy could reply she had run across the room towards Lord Wymonde.

After kissing him good-night, she disappeared from the Ball-Room.

"I am sorry, Your Highness," Lucy said to the Prince.

"So very young and enchantingly elusive," he murmured.

Lucy was not quite certain what he meant by that and was not interested.

She had already held out her arms to the Marquis, and as the music started again they were dancing.

He wondered vaguely as she pressed herself as close to him as she dared, whether he might suggest they could visit the Conservatory, but decided it was too obvious.

Besides he had the uncomfortable feeling, although he was not certain why, that George Wymonde was regarding him in a somewhat hostile fashion.

"I have done nothing wrong," he told himself, as if he had been accused unjustly, but Lucy's face raised to his was very revealing.

Riding across the Park he thought over the plan he had made to amuse his guests this afternoon, tomorrow there would be a local point-to-point, and on Tuesday they would return to London.

It was, the Marquis suddenly thought, the type of programme that had been repeated and repeated year after year, with only a few items changed according to the different seasons.

In the winter there would be shooting on Saturdays, and a dance in the evening, another big shoot on Monday, and of course, every evening dinner-parties with very much the same people as tonight.

When it was really hot in July they would sometimes take a picnic to the Folly, built by his grandfather, which stood on the highest point of the estate.

There would be a visit, either riding or driving, to the ruined Abbey that was locally reputed to be haunted.

There was nothing new, but really, the Marquis thought, there was nothing else to do but carry out the programme of last year and the year before that.

He rode over one of the two bridges that spanned the lake.

Now he was in the gardens that swept down from the great house and which had been added to and improved by every owner of Chale until they rivalled the gardens at Kew.

Close to the lake his grandfather had planted two acres of ground with almond trees.

They were breathtakingly beautiful when they came into flower at this time of the year, and when the Marquis rode early before the rest of his guests were awake, he always returned home through the almond trees.

He could see now their pink and white blossom as he rode towards them and he could not believe there could be anywhere in the world more beautiful.

Then, as he reached the first of the trees and drew in his horse to admire the vista of them sloping slightly up an incline towards the shrubs of the lilac garden, he saw that he was not alone in what was a Paradise of blossom.

Moving under the trees was someone in white, and as the Marquis recognised Ina, he wondered what she was doing.

Then he saw as he peered through the blossom-covered branches of the trees, that she was dancing.

Because she was so graceful she seemed amongst the petals falling from the trees to be the very personification of spring.

For a moment the Marquis could hardly believe

that she was real and not just a figment of his imagination.

She was wearing pink, and her face was turned upwards towards the trees. Her arms were bare and she moved them as a ballerina might have done with the same poise and the same poetry of movement that seemed part of the vibrations coming from the earth itself.

Her feet hardly seemed to touch the ground as she twirled and danced in and out of the tree-trunks, twisting her way downwards and coming quite unconsciously nearer and nearer the Marquis.

Then before she reached him, the dance which seemed as if she moved to music only she could hear, came to an end.

She sank down on the dry grass with her back against the trunk of a tree.

The Marquis could see quite clearly that she was smiling and as a petal touched her cheek as it fell, she held out both her hands, palms upwards, to catch any others.

The Marquis dismounted and knotting the reins over his horse's neck he left him free knowing as there was so much fresh grass to eat, that he would not wander far.

Then he walked towards Ina.

She was looking upwards through the blossom above her and the sky peeping through it, and she was not aware of him until he stood beside her.

Then as if she came back to earth from some magical world as she looked at him, her eyes were a little bemused and she did not speak.

The Marquis lowered himself down on the grass

beside her, his highly polished riding-boots shining in the morning sun.

"Last night," he said in his deep voice, "you told me that I might be Kubla Khan. Now I have some more lines to add to those which described my 'stately pleasure-dome.'"

Ina smiled, and he thought as she did so, that her skin must have the same softness as a petal which had just fallen on his hand.

He did not wait for her to say anything, but recited:

"A thousand fragrant petals fell
On a nymph, a sprite, whose dancing will
Lift my heart to Heaven from Hell
Whenever I remember."

Ina gave a little cry and clapped her hands together.

"That is lovely! You are a poet!"

"You brought those lines to my mind," the Marquis replied, "but I have not had time to polish them."

"They are perfect just as they are," she said. "You have written poetry before?"

"A long time ago when I was at Oxford," the Marquis confessed, "I fancied myself as another Lord Byron, but there was no chance of my becoming famous overnight!"

"That is not important," Ina said. "You wrote what you felt you had to express, and that is what matters."

She felt he did not understand and said:

"Papa never tried to sell his pictures and never wanted to exhibit them. He painted them because he felt what he had seen had to be captured, and he said once he was making time stand still for one minute in eternity."

"I have not felt like that since I left Oxford, and became busy in the more mundane world," the Marquis smiled.

"I do not think that is true," Ina replied.

"What do you mean by that?"

"I think that if you have poetry in you, you have felt it and been aware that you should express it. That you have not done so hurt you and perhaps the world to whom you might have given something important."

The Marquis looked at her in surprise, but once again she was looking up at the blossom overhead.

There was a faint breeze and now more petals were falling, and as they lay on Ina's fair hair and on her shoulders, the Marquis knew that the picture she made could only be expressed in poetry.

She must have known what he was thinking because she said quietly:

"Just now those beautiful words came to your mind and I cannot believe there have not been many, many times in your life when the words have been there, but you have not written them down as you should have done."

"Are you taking me to task?" the Marquis asked.

"I think you have missed opportunities that may never come again."

Now the Marquis was astonished.

It had been a long time since a woman had criticised him, except when he had made it clear that he was no longer interested in her.

How could this child say that he had wasted his opportunities when he had most admirably filled his position in the County, at Court, and of course, in Society, in a manner that had earned him compliments not only from women, but also from men much older than himself?

He was wondering how he could tell Ina that she was completely wrong when she said:

"I think perhaps you have lost your way because you have been complacent and therefore lost the excitement of surprise."

"I am certainly not admitting that!" the Marquis said sharply.

Then he knew that Ina was not listening, but following a mental path of her own, or rather of his, in a concentrated manner which made him feel almost as if she was looking back into his past with an inner perception that might be clairvoyance.

"Even the most perfect and beautiful things can become too familiar," she said softly. "That is why one should always climb mountains, either physically or metaphorically. When one reaches the top there is another mountain, or as Papa would have said another horizon, and beyond that, yet another."

"You really think all that exploring would make me happy?" the Marquis asked.

"I think you would find yourself," Ina answered.

The Marquis felt almost as if she had caught him in a spell, and because he was nervous of what she was doing to him, he said mockingly:

"You talk as though you are looking into a magic

crystal-ball, or perhaps reading my fortunes by the cards."

Ina did not seem to mind the fiery manner in which he spoke. She merely answered:

"I suppose in a way you are right. That is what I am doing. But I do not need a crystal-ball, or even a magic one."

"Then what do you need?"

She turned to smile at him and he thought the sunlight was caught in her eyes.

"Just as Papa had his paintings and you have your poetry, so I also have a way of expression for what I feel and think."

"And what is that?"

"I think perhaps I should make you guess, because I have a feeling that your instinct has grown a little rusty."

Now she was laughing at him and it was certainly a new experience for the Marquis.

At the same time he found the dimple beside her mouth gave her a mischievous look that had not been there before.

As if he told himself it was a childish game in which he must take part, he thought for a moment. Then he said:

"You are musical. When you were dancing just now I thought you were listening to the music of the spheres."

"That is true," Ina said without showing any self-consciousness, "but music is not the way I express myself."

"Then what is?" the Marquis asked. "Tell me."

She hesitated, and he added quickly:

"Just as we agreed last night, anything you tell

me is secret and will not be repeated."

"That is what I wanted you to say."

"I hope I was using my instinct."

"Or reading my thoughts."

"That is something I shall certainly try to do," he answered. "But tell me the answer to your puzzle."

"The way I express myself is rather strange," Ina said, "and perhaps it is a little unfair to expect you to guess it."

She paused for a moment before she said:

"I cannot paint things as Papa did, but I try to draw and I find it interesting to set down the different types of people I have seen and met all over the world."

"I should be most interested to see your sketches, if you will show them to me."

"You might be insulted."

"Why?" he enquired.

"Because when I draw people my pencil, in some strange way which I do not consciously control, portrays not only their character, but either what they are or what they should be."

Ina made a little gesture with her hands as she went on:

"It is rather difficult to explain, but when I drew an Arab Chieftain he was expecting me to show him in all his tribal glory. But when the sketch was finished it was of a man completely naked, holding out his arms to the sky as if he was begging for help."

The Marquis listened in astonishment. Then he asked:

"You have drawn me?"

Ina nodded.

"And how did your pencil show me?"

"Perhaps I should not tell you this, but I think after what you have just been saying you will understand."

"I shall try to bear it, however hard it may be," the Marquis replied.

"I thought that I would draw you as a King, as I thought you first were, perhaps even as Kubla Khan."

"And was I a native beggar?" the Marquis asked, an undoubted note of sarcasm in his voice.

Again Ina shook her head.

"No," she replied, "you were a pilgrim sitting by the roadside with your back to the mountains towards which you had been travelling."

There was a silence. Then the Marquis said:

"Are you telling me the truth?"

Ina did not bother to reply. She merely turned her head to look at him and he saw the answer in her eyes.

"You could not have known we were going to have this conversation," he said.

"I had no idea that you could write poetry," Ina replied. "In fact I admired you so tremendously because you were part of Chale that what I drew surprised me no less than it had surprised you."

"I am certainly extremely surprised," the Marquis said indignantly. "If you drew me as a pilgrim, then what am I seeking? What am I trying to find?"

He thought, as he spoke, of Chale, of his great possessions, and once again of his unassailable position in the Social World.

"The truthful answer to that," Ina said softly, "is very simple. We are all seeking ourselves, and in the fulfilment of ourselves—happiness."

As if her words and the way she spoke had moved him, the Marquis felt that he must break the spell that he felt with some alarm, she had cast over him.

He wanted to get away. He wanted to escape from all the thoughts she had evoked in him which he felt were sweeping aside his contentment, and in fact, his complacency.

He rose to his feet.

"It is getting late," he said, "and quite frankly I am feeling hungry."

She did not answer and he had moved away from her before he looked back to see that she was once again looking up towards the sky.

He had the feeling that she had forgotten him.

He wanted to ask her if she was coming back to the house, but as it seemed such a senseless question he walked on towards his horse.

He mounted, and as he rode away he looked once again at Ina.

She was where he had left her, but he would not have been in the least surprised if she had vanished, and he had imagined her and their whole conversation.

"Dammit all!" he complained in an irritated manner. "She is far too unpredictable for a girl of her age!"

He had a longing to get back to the sanity of a prosaic English breakfast, and a conversation about horses with his male guests.

"The whole thing was a lot of mumbo-jumbo

nonsense!" he said aloud.

Even as he spoke the words he knew they were a lie.

Lord Wymonde walked into his wife's bedroom where she was sitting up in bed finishing her breakfast.

She wore a little lace cap on her fair hair, and a dressing-jacket trimmed with lace and bows of velvet ribbon. She looked entrancing.

She had however no smile for her husband because, as she had often said, breakfast was the one meal she ate alone, and she liked it to be in peace.

"What is it, George?" she asked in a somewhat querulous tone.

"You are going to be rather annoyed, my dear," Lord Wymonde replied, "but I have had a letter from Lord Marlow, more or less demanding that I go there tonight to a dinner-party that is to be given for the Chairman of the Jockey Club."

"Tonight?" Lucy queried.

"It means we need not leave here until after tea."

"*We?*" Lucy echoed, her voice rising a little on the one syllable.

"He has naturally asked you, my dear."

"I have no intention of accepting Lord Marlow's invitation, and I consider it insulting to be asked at the last moment!"

Lord Wymonde glanced down at the letter in his hand.

"Marlow explains that quite easily," he said.

"Apparently there is a controversial question coming up at the Jockey Club meeting which takes place on Thursday, and it is absolutely essential that the older members should have a chance of discussing beforehand what action should be taken."

"Horses! Horses!" Lucy exclaimed. "Do men ever talk about anything else? Well, of course, George dear, you must go, but there is no need for me to be bored to distraction by your endless chatter on the subject."

Her voice was almost spiteful.

Like all women she always resented with a kind of inborn jealousy her husband's preoccupation and absorbing interest in anything that was not herself.

"Are you saying you are not coming with me?" Lord Wymonde asked.

"Let me make it very clear, George," Lucy replied. "It is quite impossible for me to come with you when there is a special dinner-party planned for tonight to which all our greatest friends have been invited, besides some young men for Ina."

She saw her husband was partially convinced by this argument, and added quickly:

"Now we have a young girl to consider, it is very important for her to consolidate the friendships she has already made at the dance. In fact, I thought Lord Fleet was definitely interested and, as you well know, he is an extremely eligible young man."

"For goodness sake, Lucy, give the child a chance to look around before you marry her off to the first man she meets."

Lucy suppressed a desire to reply: "The sooner the better!" but said instead:

"You must admit, I have done my very best for your niece so far. She has met more attractive unmarried men here at Chale than she is ever likely to meet in one evening in a London Ball-Room. Lord Fleet, as I have already said, and that handsome Branscombe boy, are both very eligible."

"I am not saying that eventually it might not be a bad idea for her to marry either of them," Lord Wymonde conceded, "but do not push her, Lucy. I will not have Roland's daughter forced to marry any man, unless she wishes to do so."

Lucy opened her eyes wide and managed to look extremely surprised.

"As if I would think of doing anything so unkind!" she protested. "I am only thinking of little Ina, as you asked me to do."

Now there was a plaintive note in her voice, which her husband was well aware was a danger-signal.

"Yes, yes, my dear. Of course you are doing the right thing," he said quickly. "If you are quite certain you do not mind my going to the Marlows alone, I will leave after tea, and be back first thing in the morning before you are ready to leave for London."

"There will be no hurry," Lucy answered. "I have already told Alice that we will catch the afternoon train, and she is delighted that we can stay for luncheon."

"Then that is settled," Lord Wymonde said. "I will make arrangements to leave at about five."

"I am sure you will enjoy the dinner."

There was now a note in his wife's voice that

made Lord Wymonde stop in his tracks as he was moving towards the door.

He turned and walked back towards the bed.

"Mind you behave yourself in my absence," he said. "If you ask me, Chale is far too familiar with you. If I have any trouble with him, I warn you this will be the last time you will ever stay here!"

"George!"

Lucy's exclamation was one of shock, horror, and indignation.

"How can you say such things to me! As if I have behaved with anything but the greatest propriety from the moment we arrived!"

"I do not like the way he looks at you," Lord Wymonde insisted.

Lucy shrugged her shoulders in an affected gesture which she imagined was very French.

"My dear George! You should be used to the way men look at me by this time. I cannot help it if they are bowled over by my beauty, as you were a long time ago."

She thought Lord Wymonde would respond, but when he did not, she added plaintively:

"I think you are very unkind and unjust! If I have been nice to Irvine Chale it has only been to persuade him that it was no trouble to have your niece here at short notice, and also to encourage him to invite young men to amuse her who would never ordinarily come to the house. I thought you would be grateful."

Lucy appeared as if she was going to burst into tears at any moment, and George Wymonde said quickly:

"All right! All right! I spoke hastily. After all, I am jealous, I suppose. Forgive me."

Lucy gave him a tremulous little smile.

"I will forgive you, dear George, but you must not think such unkind things about me. You know there is no man in my life apart from you, and there never has been!"

Lord Wymonde was aware that this was true. Lucy had always been a cold woman, and no one knew that better than he did.

He bent over the bed to kiss her cheek.

"You are too lovely, that is the trouble."

"I want you to be proud of me, George."

"I am," he replied.

He went from the room with a smile on his face, and only as the door shut behind him did Lucy clasp her hands together and there was a radiant expression in her eyes.

This was what she had hoped and prayed for, and now suddenly, when she least expected it, it had happened.

She gave a little sigh and lay back against her pillows. There was an expression in her eyes and a smile on her lips which many men had desired to see there, but had always been disappointed.

At dinner that night, Ina found herself seated, as she had been the first evening, beside Mr. Trevelyn.

He had always been very pleasant to her, and if he saw her alone he would always go and talk to her himself, or find somebody else to do so.

He acted, she thought, rather as if he was assistant host to the Marquis, and it was only this evening when she was dressing for dinner that she learnt to her astonishment what his position in the household really was.

She was talking to Hannah about the dinner-party.

"Aunt Lucy says Lord Fleet has been invited especially for me," she said, "but to tell you the truth, Hannah, I find him a rather boring young man."

"They say he has a very fine estate not far from here," Hannah answered.

"I think from the way Aunt Lucy spoke," Ina said ruminatively, "she was hoping Lord Fleet would fall in love with me, but I shall do everything I can to prevent him from doing anything of the sort!"

"Now don't you go making up your mind too quickly about a young man," Hannah admonished. "I'm not saying His Lordship is 'Mr. Right,' but you'll have to marry sooner or later, and I'd like to see you in your own house and wearing the robes of a Peeress."

Ina laughed.

"Oh, Hannah, you've become a real snob since we came to Chale," she teased. "I am quite certain you are not thinking of my happiness, but of your position downstairs if I wear a coronet!"

"That's not true, Miss Ina, and you know it!" Hannah said sharply. "I want you to find the happiness your father and mother had together, but I also wants you to have a home that's there to come beck to, if you ever go a-wandering."

Ina was aware that Hannah had always resented the fact that they never went back to the same place or, if they did, it was not to the same house.

As she had said, she longed for a home, and that, Ina thought, was what she wanted herself, but it depended very much with whom she shared it.

She thought of Lord Fleet and made a tiny grimace knowing she would no more marry him than try to fly to the moon.

Then she thought of the Prince, and gave a shudder.

She was astute enough to realise that he had been doing everything possible to get her alone, and she was quite certain he would try to touch her.

She had managed so far to circumvent him very cleverly.

She thought now that rather than marry some elderly man who was grasping at her because she was young and he saw in her the echo of his own youth, she would rather remain unmarried all her life.

"I think Aunt Lucy wants to be rid of me," she said aloud, "but I swear to you, Hannah, I will never marry to please her or anyone else, but only when my heart tells me that he is the one man in the world for me."

She gave a little sigh and added:

"But perhaps he will not feel the same about me."

There was something wistful about the last words, but Hannah, who had gone to the wardrobe to collect her gown, did not hear them.

It was silly of her, Ina thought, but she had felt

hurt yesterday, and again today because the Marquis had not come near her, and she was quite sure that he was deliberately avoiding her.

She could not understand why, and when she thought back over the conversation they had had under the almond trees it was difficult to know why he should be angry with her.

"It was foolish of me to tell him about my drawing," she chided herself, "but in a way I cannot explain, I wanted to tell him the things I have never told anyone else except Papa."

She knew if she was honest that she wanted to talk to him and had no wish to talk to any other man in the house-party.

Perhaps it was presumptuous, perhaps it was asking too much, but she felt as though not only was the Marquis interesting, but something within her reached out towards him.

Intuitively she was aware that he understood what she was trying to say when no one else could.

"I want to talk to him," she thought. "I know he is busy, I know he is the host, I know he has a thousand things to see to, but there must have been a moment when we could be together."

Then she told herself that was asking too much.

The Marquis had all the older ladies to look after who she was certain were very demanding.

There was not only Aunt Lucy, who seemed to grow lovelier each day, but that nice Mrs. Marshall, and the dark-eyed Countess who seemed to belong to the Prince when he was not pursuing her.

There were half-a-dozen other ladies with beautiful faces, exquisite figures and clothes so elaborate and elegant that Ina sometimes had the impression she was dressed in rags.

How could she possibly try to compete with the sophistication of the beauties who were acclaimed throughout the length and breadth of the British Isles?

"If I am seated next to Lord Fleet at dinner," she said aloud, "I hope that nice Mr. Trevelyn is on my other side. He always seems to be interested in everything I have to say."

"It's no use setting your cap at him!" Hannah said grimly. "He's fully booked, as you must have realised by now."

"What do you mean by that?" Ina asked.

"He's the Marchioness's pet. Goes everywhere with her, waits on her hand and foot. They tell me downstairs he's the best of all the gentlemen she's had in tow."

Ina drew in her breath.

She was well aware why Hannah was telling her this—in case she should waste her time thinking of Mr. Trevelyn as a young man for herself.

It was actually an idea that had never entered her mind. She thought of him as quite old.

Of course he was by no means as old as her father or the Prince, but he had been kind and considerate to her the first night she had arrived, when it had all been rather awe-inspiring.

That he should be, as Hannah had said the property of the Marchioness who seemed very, very old, was something she had never anticipated or imagined was possible.

Now, almost as if Hannah had opened her eyes,

she saw how the house-party with the exception of herself, had been paired off.

There was the Marchioness and Mr. Trevelyn, there was the Prince and the dark-eyed lady, who watched him with smouldering eyes whatever he was doing, and there were several other couples who always seemed to be talking to someone who was not their wife or their husband.

And the Marquis?

He was paired with nobody. How could he be? Ina thought with a lift of her heart, and it was obvious that if the pattern was to be completed she should be paired with him.

"I like him! I like him very much!" she told herself, and felt an overwhelming eagerness to go downstairs to see him again.

"I want to talk to him," she added, "and perhaps he has written me another poem."

She had managed to remember and write down the lines he had said to her, and as a few minutes later she was going down the stairs, not bothering to wait for Aunt Lucy who would be late so that she could make an entrance at the last moment, Ina repeated to herself the words the Marquis had said to her in his deep voice:

". . . a nymph, a sprite, whose dancing will
Lift my heart to Heaven from Hell
Whenever I remember . . ."

"I would like to do that for him," Ina whispered, "but could I really do anything so wonderful?"

There was no answer!

Chapter Five

THE MARQUIS was well aware by the expression on Lucy's face that she had something important to tell him.

"I must speak to you alone," she whispered after luncheon.

He wondered what was making her look so happy.

She had not been seated next to him during the meal because one of the guests was the Lord Lieutenant's wife who had to be on his right, and the Countess, as was correct in precedence, was on his left.

It had been for the Marquis a rather boring two hours, because the Lord Lieutenant's wife was a dictatorial woman who voiced her opinions insistently and had no wish to be contradicted by anyone.

He therefore found himself thinking of what Ina had said to him yesterday and it still annoyed him because it made him, he found, critical of everything that was happening.

Always in the past he had thought himself to be proud of and pleased by the clockwork efficiency with which everything happened at Chale, like a play that had run for hundreds of nights, and was therefore almost perfect.

"Why should I want anything else?" the Marquis asked.

He looked at servants moving silently round the table offering the guests excellently cooked dishes on the crested silver and replenishing the crystal wine-glasses.

He knew even as he asked the question that what Ina had been talking about was far more subtle and, although he would not admit it, far more intriguing.

It was his mind that she queried, and he knew that the reason for his recently finding himself bored and increasingly cynical was that he had not had enough demands made on him to keep his brain stimulated to new efforts.

"I am content exactly as I am!" the Marquis tried to tell himself angrily.

He knew it was untrue, yet because he had no wish to hear any more from Ina he concentrated his attentions on Lucy.

He kept telling himself that she was the most beautiful woman he had ever seen, and it was certainly an achievement to have brought a light to her eyes that no man had been able to do before, and to know that when he touched her a thrill made her quiver.

He glanced around the Drawing-Room and seeing that the Lord Lieutenant's wife was laying down the law to Harry Trevelyn and everyone else appeared after such a good luncheon to be talking animatedly to one another, he answered Lucy by saying:

"Let us walk into the garden. It will be easier there."

She smiled at him and he turned to his nearest guest who was a neighbouring hunting Squire to say:

"I expect you would like to see the horses, Garfield. I have several new additions to my stables since you were last here."

"So I have learned from my grooms, who are filled with envy."

"Then do go to the stables," the Marquis said. "You know the way, and I will join you in a few minutes."

His friend, as the Marquis had anticipated, asked the lady to whom he was talking if she would accompany him, and it was then easy for the Marquis and Lucy to follow them.

But while his two guests walked in the direction of the stables, Lucy and the Marquis moved behind a high yew hedge towards the Herb Garden.

As soon as they were out of sight of the house Lucy said:

"Has George told you?"

"Told me what?" the Marquis enquired.

"He has to stay with Lord Marlow tonight."

"I have not seen George since I came back from riding."

"He will be leaving after tea," Lucy said. "He wanted me to go with him, but I refused."

"I am glad about that."

"Are you really glad?"

"Do I have to put what is very obvious into words?"

Lucy smiled at him and looked so lovely as she did so that he told himself words were completely unimportant.

"I have never seen you look so beautiful!" the Marquis said, and she thought his voice had deepened.

Then as they stood still looking at one another he added:

"I will tell you how beautiful tonight, but now we must join the others."

Lucy did not protest. She had learned all she wanted to know, and although horses bored her to distraction she was prepared to look at them as long as she could be beside the Marquis and feel that he was as conscious of her as she was of him.

When George joined them a few minutes after they arrived at the stables she managed to give him a welcoming smile before she was annoyed to see that he had brought Ina with him.

"I thought you did not care for horses," George said in what was a rather disagreeable voice. "You certainly never visit the stables at home!"

There was a little frown between Lucy's eyes,

but she forced herself to slip her arm through her husband's and drew him to one side.

"Where is Lord Fleet?" she asked in a low voice so that no one else could hear what she said. "I left him talking to Ina."

"He has left," Lord Wymonde replied, "and he asked me to apologise to Alice and the Marquis, who had quite unaccountably disappeared."

Lucy heard the suspicion in her husband's voice that was definitely a warning that he was going to be difficult, and she was suddenly afraid that he might change his mind and say he would not go away.

"Oh, dear, how disappointing!" she said aloud. "I had hoped that he would make some effort to try to see Ina again, but I dare say we will be able to inveigle him to a dinner-party in London."

George was still looking disagreeable, but Lucy moving a little closer to him, said:

"I am trying to please you, George. I am really!"

The words sounded sincere, and she looked so lovely that Lord Wymonde found it was impossible to do anything but smile.

"Thank you, Lucy," he said, "and I am grateful, my dear."

"Let us go back to the house together," Lucy suggested. "I hate walking on these cobbles. They hurt my feet, but when I was asked to come to the stables I did not like to refuse."

She did not give George a chance to say anything sarcastic and chatted to him all the way back to the house, content in one way because Ina had come back with them, and not stayed behind with the Marquis and his friends.

She told herself the child looked very out of place at a party where everyone was older and more sophisticated.

But she knew in fact, Ina in her white gown just looked young, like the flowers coming into bloom and the syringa which scented the air.

Their fragrance made Lucy think of orange blossom, and she told herself that she would get Ina married one way or another, before the Season was over.

"I must find out from George how much money she has," she thought. "It will make things so much easier if she has a decent income to offer a prospective husband."

They reached the house to find the last of the luncheon guests were saying good-bye.

As soon as the Marchioness was alone Lord Wymonde took the opportunity to tell her that he had unfortunately to leave immediately after tea, to stay with Lord Marlow.

"Oh, George, how tiresome of you!" the Marchioness exclaimed. "Now you will upset the table for dinner and I was so looking forward to your sitting next to me."

"It is my loss," Lord Wymonde said gallantly. "But you know only too well what Edward Marlow is like when there is some difficulty in the Jockey Club."

"I do indeed!" the Marchioness agreed, "and of course, you must go, but you are not taking dear Lucy with you?"

"No, I am leaving her in your charge," Lord Wymonde replied, "and of course Ina."

"Lord Fleet says he cannot dine with us tonight,"

Alice announced, "but Charles Branscombe is coming, and I am sure Ina will find him very charming and intelligent."

Ina did not answer, but she had already danced with Charles Branscombe and as he was very conceited and puffed up with his own importance, she thought that on the whole she preferred Lord Fleet.

However there was nothing she could do but say to the Marchioness how kind it was of her to take so much trouble for her, while she was perfectly happy just to be at Chale.

"We like having you here," the Marchioness said, "and you must do everything today that has to be done before you leave us tomorrow."

"I have seen nearly all the house," Ina said.

"Do not forget the Orangery," the Marchioness admonished. "That was built long before the rest of the building."

"I should be delighted to show such a lovely young lady the Orangery, or anywhere else," a voice said beside Ina and she started as she realised it was the Prince.

"Thank you," she said, "it is very kind of Your Highness, but at the moment I have to go upstairs and get a handkerchief which I have forgotten."

It was a poor excuse but it enabled Ina to escape from the Prince, and as she ran up the stairs she told herself it was a nuisance because she had been looking forward to seeing the Orangery, but she had no intention of going there with him.

As was usual at Chale, time passed quickly, because meal followed meal—and it was expected that the ladies should change their gowns at least four times a day.

Lucy came down to tea looking ravishing in a lighter and more elaborate creation than she had worn at luncheon and Ina had changed into one of white lace threaded through with very narrow blue velvet ribbon which ended in front with tiny bows and in larger ones at the back.

It was an expensive French gown and she had wondered until now, whether she would ever have an opportunity of wearing it.

But as Mrs. Harvester had insisted on buying it because she thought it so pretty, Ina could not understand why Lucy looked at her with an obvious expression of disapproval.

Tea was a ritual meal with the Marchioness presiding over a table laden with a fantastic display of silver tea-pot, kettle, milk and cream jugs, sugar-basin and tea-strainer, and so many different things to eat that it was impossible, Ina thought, that anyone could be hungry for dinner.

After tea the ladies gossiped while the gentlemen went to the Billiard-Room, either to challenge each other to an expensive game of Pool, or to snooze in the big comfortable leather arm-chairs.

Ina went up to her bedroom to read a novel which she had taken from the Library.

Although it was interesting, she found herself thinking of the Marquis and wondering if after tomorrow she would ever see him again.

She had been disappointed that he had not asked to look at her sketch-book and she thought it strange that he had not been curious to see how she had drawn him.

She opened her book and turned the pages to look at her drawing of him, not understanding what had happened.

She had been quite certain that the Marquis would appear as a King or Kubla Khan in his "stately pleasure dome."

But the pilgrim sitting at the side of the road with his back to the mountain undoubtedly had the features and the expression of the Marquis.

Indisputably it was a true and revealing portrait, and however much the Marquis might protest, she had portrayed him as he actually was.

"I should not have told him about it," she thought a little unhappily, and shut the sketch book with a snap.

Dinner followed the same pattern as it had for the last three nights with the exception that there was a different arrangement of orchids on the table, and different neighbours had been invited to swell the house-party.

Charles Branscombe was even more cocksure than he had been the last time Ina had talked to him.

He obviously thought it was a bore to be sitting next to anyone so young, and as there were a lot of beautiful women present, Ina was sure that he longed to dance attendance upon them, so that he could tell his friends what a success he was.

She had no wish to talk to him, and instead engaged the gentleman on her other side in a long discussion on the difference between French and Italian food.

She gathered he was a gourmet, and as she had

spent a lot of time in both countries they were able to compare notes over different dishes and argue over the merits of the Chefs in Paris and in Rome.

"You are too young to be interested in food," Ina's companion said, "and I am surprised at your very extensive knowledge of it."

"My father was very particular about what he ate," Ina replied. "He said it was important that one should appreciate the food of the country rather than demand eggs and bacon and apple-dumplings if one was English, or an endless diet of spaghetti because one was Italian."

Ina's companion laughed.

"And what sort of food do you prefer?"

"I find Moroccan enjoyable," Ina replied because she was sure it would involve an argument.

When dinner was over and they moved to the Drawing-Room, the older members of the party began to play cards, and Ina saw the Marquis was talking to Aunt Lucy.

They were standing against a background of blue brocade curtains with exquisitely draped pelmets edged with a deep fringe.

She thought how attractive they both looked, with Aunt Lucy's diamonds glittering on her golden hair and found her long beck and making her look like a Fairy Queen.

"She is so beautiful!" Ina thought admiringly. "It is sad for her to have to grow old and look like the Marchioness, who must also have been very lovely when she was young."

She knew how hard her aunt worked to keep her beauty.

She had seen an enormous array of lotions, pomades and ointments on Lucy's dressing-table, and she knew that her lady's maid massaged her face and while she was resting put pads of cotton-wool dipped in witchhazel on her closed eyes.

"It is a losing battle, because eventually she will grow old, her face will become lined and her hair go grey," Ina thought.

She remembered that Mrs. Harvester had looked beautiful even though she was over seventy.

There had been such a kind, sweet expression on her face, and she had been interested in so many different things that she never appeared to think about herself.

"That is what I must try to be like," Ina thought and started when the man who was sitting beside her asked:

"What can I have said to make you look so serious?"

The evening ended rather earlier than usual because there was no dancing, and some of the guests were obviously not interested in cards.

Ina noticed that at least one person never moved from the card-tables, and that was the Prince. She thought therefore with satisfaction that she had managed to keep out of his way the whole day.

At the same time she was glad when she could go up to bed, remembering the book that she had been reading and realising that if she did not finish it now she would never know the ending.

"I will finish it tonight," she promised herself, and undressed hurriedly and got into bed.

For a moment her eyes went to her sketch-book which stood on the table where she had left it.

She thought she would take another peep at her portrait of the Marquis then determinedly she opened her novel.

If Ina thought the evening had passed quickly, Lucy felt very differently.

For her the dinner had dragged on interminably, and she found herself wanting to scream at the visitors that it was time for them to leave.

It was in fact, because she yawned and made a rather obvious attempt to hide it with her hand that the elderly gentleman to whom she was talking said:

"I think you must be tired, Lady Wymonde, and it is time we should be going. We have a long drive home."

"It is wise not to leave too late," Lucy agreed quickly. "I am always terrified if the horses go too fast in the dark in case one should have an accident."

"You are quite right. It can be dangerous," the gentleman replied.

He walked across the Drawing-Room to tell his wife they should be on their way.

Lucy kissed the Marchioness good night and thanked her effusively for such a wonderful evening.

Then as she laid her long thin fingers in the Marquis's hand her eyes met his, and he saw there was undoubtedly a little flicker of fire in their blue depths.

Upstairs Lucy found her tired maid waiting up as usual, to undress her.

As her elaborate décolleté gown was unbuttoned at the back, the tight corsets that came from France unlaced, her silk stockings gently rolled down over her well-shaped legs and slim ankles she hardly noticed what was happening.

Her maid brought her one of her exquisite lace nightgowns, but she demanded an even more ornate one, and the négligée that matched it was a new acquisition of blue satin with frill upon frill of expensive lace, round both the neck and the hem.

The wide sleeves were also trimmed with lace to fall back to reveal Lucy's hands which she moved with a grace that she had assumed after dozens of lessons in deportment.

The whiteness of her skin was something she had been born with, and she knew that no colour accentuated it better than the blue which matched her eyes and which she habitually wore.

"Shall I brush your hair, M'Lady?" the maid asked.

"Yes, but not a hundred strokes tonight," Lucy answered. "Just twenty, then twist my hair into a knot with several large hair-pins to hold it."

She gave a little secret smile at herself as she spoke, remembering how many men had said to her:

"I want to release your lovely hair from the pins which confine it, my darling, see it fall over your white shoulders, and kiss you through it as if it was a veil."

It was something she had never allowed any of them to do.

But tonight would be different.

With a rising excitement she thought of how the Marquis's hands would draw the pins from her hair and before he held her lips captive he would kiss her through the veil of her hair.

"I love him!" Lucy told her reflection in the glass.

No man had ever made her feel as she felt now.

"I have caught him!" she went on in her mind. "Caught the most elusive and irresistible bachelor in the whole of London, and having done so I will make certain he does not escape me!"

"Are you getting into bed, M'Lady?" the maid asked.

Lucy realised that the woman had finished what she was doing.

"No, not yet," she replied. "But you can leave me now. Blow out all the candles except for those by the bed. I wish to write a letter in my *Boudoir*."

"Very good, M'Lady."

The maid tidied the dressing-table, and as Lucy walked into the *Boudoir* she left by the other door, leaving only a candelabrum with a gold angel holding two small candles lighted on either side of the canopied bed.

It made the room look mysterious and lovely, and there was a heavy fragrance of malmaison carnations.

The maid having reached the door, took a last long look to see that nothing was forgotten.

Then as her glance fell on the bed turned back invitingly, there was a twist of her lips and an expression in her eyes which Lucy would undoubtedly have found extremely impertinent.

Lucy locked the bedroom door and waited impatiently in the *Boudoir*.

She thought she was far too clever and too subtle to be in bed when the Marquis came to her.

It would be what he would expect, and she told herself that she must go through the preliminaries of being surprised at his appearance, and of course unprepared for what they both knew was the inevitable.

Because she thought she would look like Madame Recannier she arranged herself nonchalantly on the satin-covered *chaise longue*.

She took up a book and laid it on her lap, and was poised, waiting and listening for the moment when the door would open.

───────── ◆ ─────────

The Marquis had gone to his bedroom, found his valet waiting for him and sent him to bed.

"I have several letters to write," he said, "and I may be some time . . ."

"It's no trouble, M'Lord."

"Thank you, but go to bed!" the Marquis ordered.

The valet did as he was told and the Marquis would have been surprised if he had known what the servant was thinking as he closed the bedroom door quietly behind him.

The Marquis glanced at his watch.

He knew that Lucy would have to finish with her maid, and he also knew she would take longer than he did.

He had, however, lingered downstairs for quite

a time after the ladies had gone to bed, talking to the Prince whom he considered an intelligent and interesting man when he was not running after women.

They spoke about the political situation in Russia, then as they walked up the stairs together, the Prince said:

"I find that young niece of George Wymonde's a very attractive child."

The Marquis frowned.

"She is too young for Your Highness."

It was a remark the Prince would not have allowed many of his friends to make, but he was extremely fond of the Marquis and always treated him as if he was a contemporary.

"When you get as old as I am, Chale," he said, "you will have an appreciation of certain qualities, which only the young possess."

"I am not particularly thinking of your feelings, but of hers," the Marquis replied.

The Prince smiled.

"Again when you get to my age," he answered, "you will find the stalk, however long it takes and however difficult, is the real enjoyment of the sport."

They had reached the door of the Prince's bedroom.

The Marquis had an impulse to tell him to leave Ina alone, then he told himself it was none of his business.

"Good-night, Your Highness," he said instead.

"Good-night, and thank you for a most enjoyable visit."

The Marquis walked on to his own room.

He thought now he had certainly waited long enough and he opened the door of his bedroom.

From past experience he had found in his *affaires de coeur* that it was always a mistake to assume that he was the conqueror until victory had been conceded.

This meant that he had never, the first time he had visited a woman's bedroom, arrived undressed as if assuming that she would surrender herself before she had actually done so.

He had in fact, because he was so attractive, never been refused what he sought.

But there was one famous London beauty who it was known delighted in leading a man, as it was said, "up the garden path," then slamming the gate at the very last moment, in his face.

The Marquis was sure this would never happen to him.

At the same time he remembered how discomfited some of his friends had been when they had arrived at the bedroom of the lady in question, either to find the door was locked, or to be told that they had misunderstood her feelings for them and must leave immediately in case she was compromised.

"I have never been so damned humiliated in my whole life!" one man had told the Marquis, "especially as I knew that what had happened would be repeated from *Boudoir* to *Boudoir* the following morning. I still cannot understand why she behaved like that."

"Power, my dear boy—a desire to show her power over what she contemptuously considers 'a mere man.'"

Because this had caused such an amount of talk in the Clubs, the Marquis had made sure that he would never be put in the same position.

But he felt certain of the outcome where Lucy was concerned, and that she wanted him and would be waiting for him.

Yet if the stories about her were true and she was in fact, a "glacier" then he could retreat, if that was what he should do, with dignity.

He gave a perfunctory knock on the *Boudoir* door, opening it as he did so and locking it behind him.

He appreciated immediately the picture Lucy made on the *chaise longue.*

The light gleamed on the vivid gold of her hair, masses of flowers in the background gave the appearance of a stage-set, and there was an undeniable expression of welcome on her lovely face.

He stood at the door for a moment looking at her.

Lucy had rehearsed the things she would say to him, also she would appear to be a little elusive and even reluctant to give in to his pleadings.

But when she saw him standing there looking so handsome, so magnificently masculine in his evening-clothes, all her resolutions were swept from her mind.

Without any consideration, without the slightest thought, she rose from the couch and moved towards him, her arms out-stretched before she reached him, her head thrown back, her perfect lips curved and waiting for his kisses.

Afterwards Lucy could never quite remember

how it happened, whether she had walked or the Marquis had carried her, but she was lying on the bed against her pillows, he was looking down at her, and there was no mistaking the fire in his eyes.

"I love you!" she exclaimed and the words were a cry of sheer happiness.

The Marquis pulled off his coat and threw it on the floor, to sit on the bed in front of Lucy, bending forward to kiss her again.

He pulled aside her négligée so that he could kiss her white shoulder then her neck, and it was at that moment there was a knock on the door.

For a moment Lucy could not believe she had heard it. But it came again, and a voice said:

"Lucy, let me in!"

She realised as George spoke that she had heard a slight sound before the knock as if the handle was being tried, but it had been far at the back of her mind since all she could think of was the demanding insistence of the Marquis's kisses.

She had felt they ignited a flame that was burning through her body in a way she had never experienced in the whole of her life.

She thought it would be impossible to be conscious of anything else, but now at her husband's voice she stiffened and felt as if her body had been turned to stone. She knew the Marquis felt the same.

Their eyes met and they stared at each other as if they could not believe what was happening.

Then Lord Wymonde's voice, a little louder and obviously angry repeated:

"Lucy—open the door!"

Wondering what he should do, the Marquis rose

from the bed and picked up his coat which lay on the floor.

As he put it on, he was thinking that there was a sheer drop of forty-feet outside the window, there was nowhere where a man could hide in the *Boudoir*, and on the other side of the room there was George Wymonde's dressing-room.

There was silence.

Then they both heard George Wymonde try the door of the *Boudoir*, and it flashed through Lucy's mind that the door of the dressing-room was not locked.

It was then, as the Marquis stood irresolute, that she had an idea.

No one knew better than she did that what was happening could spell complete and utter disaster not only to her marriage, but for her whole future existence.

Divorce would mean isolation and expulsion from the Social World, and she had the terrified feeling that because George had once loved her so fervently he would accuse her of adultery out of jealousy, spite, and a desire for revenge.

The handle of the *Boudoir* rattled again and Lucy, knowing now it was only a question of seconds before George thought of the dressing-room leapt from the bed.

She took hold of the Marquis by the arm and said:

"Quickly! I have an idea!"

Because for the moment his own mind was blank and he could think of nothing but the very unpleasant position in which he found himself, he followed her as she opened the communicating door between her own bedroom and her husband's dressing-room.

As George Wymonde was not expected back the room was in darkness, and without even pausing Lucy swept across the room and opened the door into Ina's bedroom.

Because there was nothing else the Marquis could do, he followed her and as they entered the room they both saw Ina sitting up in bed reading by the light of two candles.

She looked up in astonishment as they appeared.

Lucy ran to her to sit down on the mattress and pushing the novel aside took both her hands in hers.

"Ina, dearest!" she cried. "I have such an exciting, wonderful thing to tell you and I felt it would not wait until morning."

Ina looked at her wide-eyed.

Then she glanced at the Marquis as he neared the bed, looking, she thought, a little grave, but still undeniably handsome.

"What is it . . . Aunt Lucy?" she enquired.

"The Marquis, our dear host, has just told me, and I cannot express how happy it makes me, that he wishes to marry you!"

Ina started! Lucy was aware that her fingers tightened and she was very still.

There was silence, except that Lucy could faintly hear George knocking once again on her bedroom door.

"Yes, dearest Ina," she said quickly. "He has fallen in love with you, and I cannot tell you how thrilled your uncle will be, or how delighted I am, that you will be the wife of the most charming and delightful young man we have ever known."

Ina drew in her breath.

It seemed to the Marquis watching her, that her eyes seemed to fill her whole small face as she glanced up at him.

At the moment she looked not as if she was still in the schoolroom, but in the Nursery.

With her fair hair falling over her shoulders and seeming very small in the big bed that had been designed for two people she might just have been put there by an attentive Nanny.

Her nightgown, which was very pretty, had been chosen for her by Mrs. Harvester from the Convent where the Nuns made the money for their good works by selling their needlework.

It was of a very fine lawn inset with lace, which also edged the little flat collar around her neck and the frill that fell over her wrists.

It was very modest, but in the candlelight it was easy to see that although she appeared to be a little girl, her curved breasts were those of a woman nearing maturity.

Then as if the full impact of what Lucy had said was clear, Ina asked as if she spoke with the voice of an angel:

"Is it . . . true? Is it . . . really true that you . . . wish to . . . m—marry me?"

She looked at the Marquis as she spoke, and she felt as if there was no one in the room or anywhere else in the world, except him.

"I should be very honoured and proud if you

would consent to be my wife," he replied quietly.

A thousand candles seemed to have been lit behind Ina's eyes and it was at that moment that George Wymonde walked into his dressing-room and seeing the door into his niece's bedroom open, came in.

He surveyed the scene with astonishment.

Then with a most convincing cry of surprise Lucy rose from the bed on which she had been sitting and went towards him.

"George! How wonderful that you are back just when we most wanted you!" she exclaimed. "It is so exciting, and I could not bear you to miss it."

"What are you talking about? What is going on?" Lord Wymonde enquired.

He had taken in the fact that his wife was wearing a négligée with nothing beneath it but a nightgown and the Marquis was in the room. He was fully clothed, but Lord Wymonde saw that his tie was crooked and his hair a little towsled.

"Why had you locked the door of your room?" he demanded, "and what is Chale doing here?"

"That is just what I am going to tell you, George," Lucy said. "Irvine has asked for Ina's hand in marriage, and I know how delighted you will be!"

She was holding as she spoke to the revers of her husband's evening coat.

Lord Wymonde pushed her to one side, and walked to the end of Ina's bed where the Marquis was standing.

"What is all this, Chale?" he enquired. "I demand an explanation!"

It seemed for the moment as if the Marquis could not find his voice.

Then as everybody looked at him, he replied:

"I intended when you returned tomorrow George, to ask if, as Ina's Guardian, you would allow her to marry me."

He was aware that George Wymonde's eyes were searching his face, and he had the uncomfortable feeling he did not believe a word of it.

Then when Lord Wymonde was about to say something scathingly he looked towards Ina and he checked the words that were already on his lips.

It would have been impossible for anyone to look happier or more starry-eyed.

Ina had, in fact, just realised in the flash of a second that she was in love with the Marquis.

She knew now she had given him her heart from the moment their eyes met across the Dining-Room table the first night she arrived, when she had thought he looked like Kubla Khan.

She had not understood that her admiration for his appearance had been love, or that she had listened to the sound of his deep voice with love.

But when they had sat under the almond trees and talked together it had been love that she had felt flowing between them, and ever since the yearning and longing she had had to see him and to be near him was because she loved him.

Now, incredibly, wonderfully, almost as if an angel had come down from the skies to announce it, he had said he wished to marry her.

She was looking at him, and she felt as if she poured her love out towards him like the rays of the sun.

"Is this your wish?" she heard her uncle ask.

It seemed as if he was very far away and it was difficult to understand what he was saying.

With an effort she turned her face towards him.

"I asked you," Lord Wymonde said harshly, "if you really wish to marry the Marquis."

"I would . . . like it more than anything else in the whole world!" Ina answered.

Although George Wymonde was not an imaginative man he felt as if he listened to a paean of rapture like the song of the nightingales, being carried up into the sky.

He was still suspicious, still sure in his own mind that something strange was going on, but for the moment it was something he could not put into words, and certainly not in front of Ina.

"It seems to me a strange time of night to make a decision which affects your whole life," he said sourly.

"Irvine has not had an opportunity before of saying anything," Lucy interposed. "The people who were dining here only left a little while ago, and Irvine felt he must tell me what he intended before we left tomorrow."

She spoke over-insistently, and as she met his eyes Lucy knew with a stab of fear that he did not believe her.

But Ina was listening and Lord Wymonde had

no intention of letting the child be upset.

Besides, what proof had he that there was anything going on between his wife and the Marquis, except the way she was dressed and an unassailable conviction that the whole situation was false.

"Now all these dramatics are over," he said, "I suggest we go to bed and discuss this in the morning."

"I knew you would be pleased, George dearest," Lucy said. "I am so happy, so very, very happy for dear little Ina!"

She walked towards Ina as she spoke and bent and kissed her cheek, aware as she did so that she was still looking at the Marquis as if it was impossible to see anyone else.

"I am glad, if this is what you want, Ina," George Wymonde remarked, "but I can think of better and more conventional ways in which you could have received your first proposal of marriage."

There was a sting in the words which the Marquis did not miss, but Ina hardly heard him.

She was looking so radiantly happy that the light in the room seemed to come from her rather than the candles.

As if she was suddenly aware how lovely she appeared Lucy said quickly:

"Yes, of course, you are right, George. We must go to bed and we can talk it over in the morning."

"I have every intention of doing so," Lord Wymonde replied, "but I certainly need some sleep first."

He looked again at the Marquis as he spoke.

He was still staring at Ina, then as Lord Wymonde obviously waited for him to move, he said in a low voice:

"Good-night, Ina!"

"Good . . . night!"

He could hardly hear her and yet there was no need for words to express what she was feeling.

Then as the Marquis walked towards the door he passed Lord Wymonde who had his back to Ina.

For a moment the eyes of the two men met and the Marquis would have been very obtuse indeed if he had not been aware of what Lord Wymonde was thinking.

"Good-night, George!" the Marquis said.

He reached the door, opened it and went out without looking back.

Lord Wymonde turned round.

Ina was not looking at him, but in the direction where the Marquis had been when she had last seen him.

For a moment Lord Wymonde contemplated telling her what he suspected, forbidding her to marry the Marquis, and warning her that it would undoubtedly break her heart if she did so.

Yet, never a very articulate man, he knew that he could not wipe away the ecstatic look that he saw in her eyes.

He had the feeling that if he tried to do so, it would be like torturing a small animal which could not defend itself.

For better, for worse, the child he had left behind when he went away from Chale this afternoon, excited, bemused, and intrigued by the strange world around her, but not really involved in it, had now become a woman.

She still looked absurdly young, but no man, however unimaginative and prosaic, could help being aware that for the moment she radiated a love that came from her heart and her soul.

It was as perfect and ecstatic as the songs of the angels and the light that came from Heaven itself.

Lord Wymonde also had the strange feeling that for a moment he did not exist, and Ina was not even aware he was there.

He looked at her for a long moment before quietly, almost as if he was in a sacred place, he went from the room into the darkness of his own.

Chapter Six

INA AWOKE and realised with a little pang of disappointment that it was late.

She had lain awake so long last night thinking with a rapture that seemed to carry her towards the stars of the Marquis and her love for him, and it was almost dawn before she finally fell asleep with a smile on her lips.

Now, as Hannah drew back the curtains and the sun pouring golden through the windows seemed to echo the glory of her heart, she remembered that she had intended to go to the almond-trees as soon as she awoke in case the Marquis would be waiting for her there.

She felt that was the right place for them to meet

when the pink and white blossom seemed to envelop them with an unearthly beauty which made everything they said to each other seem part of a dream.

Now it was too late, and she knew he would have returned to the house, and be having breakfast downstairs.

But nothing for the moment could dim her happiness and because it seemed to be bubbling up inside her like the waters of a fountain, she sprang out of bed and ran to the window to look at the lake and the park beyond it and think it was all part of him—the man to whom she had given her heart.

She stood for some time feeling the warmth of the sun on her face, then she said as if the words came irrepressibly from between her lips:

"Oh, Hannah, I am so . . . so happy!"

"What about, except it's a nice day?" Hannah asked in her usual tart manner.

Ina drew in her breath, then turning from the window she said:

"You will hardly believe it, Hannah, but I am to . . . marry the . . . Marquis!"

The old maid stared at her for a moment as if she thought she had taken leave of her senses. Then after a perceptible pause she asked:

"What are you saying? What are you telling me, Miss Ina?"

Ina clasped her hands together and, looking like an angel in her white nightgown, moved from the window and the sunshine.

"Last night," she said in a rapt voice, "Aunt Lucy brought the Marquis in here to tell me that he wished to make me his wife!"

139

Her voice had a lilt in it as if she was almost singing the words.

Then as Hannah did not say anything she went on:

"How could I have known . . . how could I have guessed that he loved me . . . as I love him? But it is true, Hannah . . . it is true! And I am the luckiest girl in the world!"

The old maid made a strangled sound in her throat, then as she still did not speak, Ina ran to her side to say:

"Tell me you think it is wonderful, and that Mama and Papa would be pleased, as I know they would be."

"You're too young to know your own mind," Hannah answered, and there was a note in her voice that Ina did not understand.

Then it struck her that Hannah was as usual being over-protective, and she smiled tenderly as she said:

"You have always wanted me to be happy, Hannah, and I know that both you and I will be happy to live here in this wonderful house. But I keep feeling it is just a dream, and I shall wake up."

"I want your happiness, you know that, Miss Ina," Hannah said at length slowly as if she was choosing her words with care, "and being married is a big step, and something which needs thinking about."

"Not if one is in love," Ina replied, "and this has happened to me, just as it happened to Mama. She told me that when she saw Papa she knew he was the man she had dreamed about, and had always been there in her heart."

She made a little sound of sheer happiness and added:

"And that is where the Marquis has been . . . and is."

She moved around the room as if she had wings on her feet, looking at the pictures, the cupids on the corola over the bed and the inlaid furniture.

It was as if she saw them for the first time, and now they had a special significance because in the future they would belong to her as they belonged to the man who was to be her husband.

She was so wrapped up in her happiness that she did not notice the expression on Hannah's face or the apprehension in her eyes.

Nor did she have any idea with what difficulty the old woman was controlling the words which trembled on her lips, but which she dared not say.

———————◆———————

Downstairs in the Dining-Room Lord Wymonde was eating his breakfast in silence and there was a scowl on his face.

There was no sign of the Marquis, but as the male members of the house-party came into the room one after another, they were each of them surprised to see Lord Wymonde. They all made more or less the same remark.

"Hello, George! I thought you were staying with Marlow last night."

"The problem over the Jockey Club was solved

before I got there, so it was really a wasted journey," Lord Wymonde replied, not once, but half-a-dozen times.

It was obvious to them all that judging by the expression on his face whatever had occurred had upset him, so they left him alone.

When he had finished breakfast he walked from the Dining-Room into the Hall.

The Butler was there arranging the travelling-coats of the guests who would be leaving later on in the morning, and he asked:

"Is His Lordship down yet?"

"Yes, M'Lord," was the reply. "His Lordship went riding as usual before breakfast, but he's now in the Study."

Knowing where this was, Lord Wymonde walked down the passage and opened the door into a very large, comfortable room in which the Marquis usually sat when there were no guests staying in the house.

He was sitting writing at his desk and he looked up with a slightly apprehensive expression in his eyes when Lord Wymonde appeared, but he said in a perfectly calm voice:

"Good-morning, George!"

Lord Wymonde moved across the room to stand with his back to the fireplace.

"There is something I wish to say to you, Chale," he said abruptly.

The Marquis did not answer, but he put down his pen and sat back in his armchair.

"It is this," Lord Wymonde continued. "I do not

intend to talk about what occurred last night except to tell you that I will not in any circumstances, have Ina upset. I insist that if you have an engagement it will be a long one, and I shall sincerely hope that she will change her mind in the meantime."

Lord Wymonde finished speaking the words that had been barked out almost as if he was on a parade-ground.

Then as the Marquis did not reply, he added:

"That is all I have to say!"

Without looking again at his host he walked from the room, closing the door behind him.

———————————

Ina, dressed in a gown she had chosen because she thought it was the prettiest one she possessed, went down the stairs.

It was hard to have to wait while Hannah insisted that she ate some breakfast, and she thought the old maid was slower than usual in arranging her hair.

Every instinct in her body made her want to run, if she could not fly, to the Marquis's side so that he could tell her once again that he wanted to marry her. If they were alone perhaps he would take her in his arms and kiss her.

Ina drew in her breath at the thought of being close to the Marquis and feeling his lips touch hers.

It made her quiver to think of anything so wonderful, so perfect!

Just as she knew they belonged to one another and had done so since the beginning of time, so she knew that when he kissed her they would be joined indivisibly as one person, as God had meant them to be.

"I love him!" Ina said on every step of the stairs.

"I love him!" she thought, and her hand touched the bannister gently, because it was his.

She looked up at the Chale ancestors hanging on the walls and thought they smiled at her from their gilded frames, glad that she too would become one of them.

"I love him!" she wanted to cry to the footmen in the Hall.

Instead she asked demurely, feeling at the same time the colour come into her cheeks:

"Do you know where His Lordship is?"

"I don't know, Miss," the footman replied, "but I hear as he was seeing Mr. Bates in the Orangery sometime today."

Ina smiled.

"I am sure that is where I shall find him."

She started to walk quickly, wanting to run to the Orangery which she had not yet visited, but where she knew was just the place she would like to be alone with the Marquis.

Upstairs Lucy, lying back against her pillows, was facing her husband with an angry expression on her beautiful face.

She had already finished her breakfast when he came in to see her. At the same time she had known with a sinking of her heart that it was too early for what she feared would be an uncomfortable scene unless she used all her wits to prevent it.

When she left Ina's bedroom last night she had expected George would follow her to her room, but instead, somewhat to her surprise, he had stayed in his dressing-room.

When finally she had seen the light go out under the door she could hardly believe that the cross-examination she had expected had not materialised.

Now it was upon her and she wished fruitlessly that it was later in the morning when she was not feeling so tired, or although she would never have admitted it, somewhat frightened.

George's opening sentence had not been what she had expected either.

"If you hurry," he said, "we can catch the midday train with the other guests."

"Why should we want to do that?" Lucy answered. "We have already arranged that we would leave in the afternoon, but I am sure when Alice hears the news, she will want us to stay at least until tomorrow."

"I have no intention of doing any such thing!" Lord Wymonde said positively.

"But it is obvious that Alice will want us to stay."

"I do not intend to argue with you over this," Lord Wymonde said, "and if you think I will stay another night under this roof you are very much mistaken!"

There was a repressed fury in his tone that Lucy did not miss, but because he had said he did not intend to have an argument she felt some of her apprehension lift a little.

At the same time she had grown used to having her own way in everything, and George had always been very easy to handle.

"I cannot imagine," she said in a voice she forced to sound very much sweeter than she felt, "why you are taking up that attitude when you should be delighted that dear little Ina is settled for life."

There was just a quiver in Lucy's voice as she mentioned Ina's name, and a touch of spitefulness in the description which she could not have suppressed without a superhuman effort.

She then realised that her husband was staring at her in a penetrating manner that was somewhat awe-inspiring.

She looked away from him and said in a tone which had never failed to evoke a satisfactory reaction from him in the past:

"I thought you would be pleased, George. I was only trying to do what I thought was best for Ina."

Lord Wymonde made a sound that was almost derisive, and as if he could not bear to look at his wife any longer he walked across to the window to stare out with unseeing eyes.

"I am not a fool, Lucy," he said after a moment.

A wiser and cleverer woman than Lucy might have been silent. Instead she answered:

"No one is suggesting that you are, George, but it would seem not only foolish, but also rude to rush away from Chale when there is every reason why we should stay here and talk things over."

146

What Lucy was really planning in her own mind was how she could arrange to see the Marquis alone.

She was determined to talk to him, determined to make him realise that her desperate attempt to save them both from scandal was, in fact, not so upsetting as it might seem on the surface.

Last night she had lain awake thinking it over, and after a first feeling of an almost insane hatred of Ina, that she should have the Marquis as her husband, Lucy had convinced herself that it was actually almost for the best.

The Marquis would have to marry sometime, but that need not preclude his having discreet flirtations, if that was the right word for it, as did all the members of their particular set, without anyone thinking there was anything wrong about it.

The example set by the Prince of Wales had been followed by the majority of his friends and acquaintances, and Lucy was perhaps the only one of their set who had not taken a lover after being married to George for so long.

The reason was that she had not been interested in men except as admirers of her beauty, who paid her compliments as they laid their hearts at her feet.

As she had said so often and so truthfully, she had not wanted them to touch her.

But with the Marquis it was different, and she knew with a repressed fury that if George had not returned home so inopportunely and unexpectedly last night she would have sampled, for the first time, the delights of the love that her women friends had described so often.

Now they might have to wait a long time for another opportunity, but when the Marquis was engaged and eventually married to Ina there was nothing George could do to prevent their meeting continually and living, as the slang put it, "in each other's pockets."

Nothing could be better, Lucy had assured herself in the early hours of the morning, when she had lain awake turning things over and over in her mind, than that in the future George would not be able to keep her away from Chale.

She would be *persona grata* there, however difficult he might be, and Ina was certainly too young to have any say in the matter.

She told herself there would be thousands of opportunities in the future for the Marquis to tell her, as he had been trying to do last night, how beautiful she was, and how much she attracted him.

And however unpleasant George might make himself, he could not behave like a jailor twenty-four hours of the day for years on end.

"Irvine is mine, and no one else shall ever have him," Lucy vowed.

If Edwardian husbands were expected to be complacent, so were Edwardian wives, and Lucy was well aware that the more dashing of their friends left their wives in the country with the children, and only brought them to London on special occasions.

"After they are married, we will manage to be together sometimes in London, and there will certainly be occasions when I shall be able to stay at Chale alone," she told herself.

She started to count the number of race-meetings to which George would go, and to which she seldom, if ever, accompanied him.

There were those that took place in the north of England and last year he had even gone to Scotland for the game shooting.

If there was one thing Lucy really disliked it was shooting-parties where she was expected to ruin her complexion in the wind and get wet while they were waiting for birds to fly over the guns, and nothing could be more unbecoming than a cold.

The Marquis would marry Ina, Lucy argued to herself, and George would be pleased that his tiresome niece had managed to have such a brilliant marriage.

But she would hold the Marquis's heart, for no one could stop or prevent love. It was uncontrollable.

That was something that Lucy had never believed in the past, but now when she was certain she was in love she found it was exactly what the poets had written and her women friends had averred.

It was irresistible, exciting, tempestuous and wonderful.

She had always thought such descriptions were exaggerated and she had privately believed that to be demonstrative was a trifle vulgar.

Now she could understand how a woman in love could throw over everything. Not that she had any intention of doing anything so foolish, although it was only by a hair's breath that she and the Marquis had managed to escape disaster last night.

Even to think of that knock on the door and George's voice outside made Lucy feel again the fear streaking through her and the tension which had made her feel as if her body had turned to stone. It was as if everything she treasured, everything that mattered, was threatened so that it could call like a pack of cards flat on the ground around her.

Only through the sharpness of her mind and an instructive sense of self-preservation had she been able to save herself.

George had not been deceived, she knew that. At the same time, what could he do?

Lucy could only be grateful that although she had been wearing her nightgown and négligée the Marquis had been fully clothed, otherwise everything might have been more difficult.

George could think all sorts of things, but he could not prove them, and therefore it would certainly be a mistake on his part to make accusations he could not substantiate.

Lucy was in fact very sure of herself, and now she said aloud:

"Please stop being difficult, George! If we leave today I have no intention of being ready before three o'clock, which is the time I arranged originally, but it would be far better to leave tomorrow, or even the day after."

There was silence, then Lord Wymonde said, still in the harsh, uncompromising voice he had used ever since he had come to her bedroom:

"Very well, we will go at three o'clock, but no arguments from you or anyone else will persuade me to stay in this house any longer than that!"

Lucy was wondering whether her best policy would be to scream at him or cry when Lord Wymonde turned and walked from the bedroom in very much the same manner as he had left the Marquis's Study.

Ina reached the Orangery but found to her disappointment that there was no one there.

It was, however, a beautiful building and the orange trees, which she guessed were old and had been brought from Spain, were in blossom.

There were also a number of other plants and shrubs that must have come from different parts of the world, and which were not only very colourful but fascinating in that Ina had never seen them before.

She knew how much they would have interested her father and how he would have wished to paint them.

Then because it was impossible to think of anyone but the Marquis she walked to the window hoping that she might see him coming through the garden with his dogs at his heels.

She wished again that she had met him as she intended under the almond-blossom trees.

She had upset him when she told him what her drawing of him had been, but she was sure when she drew him again he would not look the same.

"I will help him to write more poems," she

thought, "and perhaps he might even try prose."

She wondered if there was a really good book on the Chaleton family and the part they had played in history, and she thought she might persuade the Marquis to write one.

She knew from the way he talked that he would not only write good English but also have a large vocabulary.

Her father had always sneered at people whose words were limited.

"The average person," he had said scornfully, "uses two to three hundred words only when there is a great wealth of language which, like music and pictures, adds to the cultivation of the mind and the development of ourselves."

When she talked to the Marquis, Ina became aware that he was not only intelligent and cultured, but he could, if he wished, also be creative on paper.

That, after all, was what her drawing had shown, and he himself had admitted it when he told her he had once written poetry.

She found herself repeating the poem he had written about her.

"... *a nymph, a sprite whose dancing will*
Lift my heart to Heaven from Hell
Whenever I remember."

She loved him and she knew that their love would make their life together a Heaven for her while she would strive in every way to make him equally happy.

He must never regret marrying her or feel that

he was missing something in life, and she was sure that being together they would find new horizons of the mind and climb new heights of intellect.

It made Ina so happy even to think of such things that she wanted to dance as she had danced under the almond trees.

"I must talk to him . . . I must see him!"

She decided to go back to the Hall to find if anyone else knew where he would be in the house or in the grounds.

Then as she turned towards the door of the Orangery she heard footsteps and thought with a leap of her heart that it was the Marquis.

She stood poised as if ready to run towards him, then as the footsteps drew nearer and a man appeared around the blossoms of an orange tree Ina saw that it was not the Marquis as she had hoped, but the Prince.

It was such a disappointment that it was like a stab of pain between her breasts.

Then for the first time she realised that she need no longer be afraid of the Prince.

She belonged to the Marquis, she was his, and that was an inviolable protection which made her safe from every other man.

She realised too, as the Prince came towards her, that he was wearing his travelling-clothes and guessed that he had sought her out so that he could say goodbye.

He glanced about him, then as he saw her standing silhouetted against some exotic plants he smiled, saying:

"I was told you were here, pretty lady, so I came

to say farewell, and tell you that as soon as you reach your uncle's house in London, I shall be calling to see you."

Ina did not speak for a moment, not certain how she should put into words what she had to tell him.

Then the Prince was beside her and he said, looking down at her:

"You are very lovely! I have a great deal to say to you that I have been unable to say here."

There was a note in his voice that was more eloquent than the words themselves, and as Ina looked up at him she saw the expression in his eyes that told her all too clearly that she had not been mistaken in what his feelings were for her.

"It is very kind of Your Highness," she said, "but I shall not be at my uncle's house for long, and while I am there I shall be very busy buying my trousseau."

The words were undoubtedly a shock, for the Prince started. Then, as if he thought he had not heard what she had said aright, he repeated:

"Your trousseau? Are you telling me you are to be—married?"

"Yes, Your Highness. I am to marry the Marquis!"

Her voice seemed to trill even as she said the words because they were so precious.

"Is this true?" the Prince asked.

"It is very true," Ina replied, "and I hope you will wish us every happiness."

She looked up at him as she spoke and was surprised by the expression she saw on his face.

Then to her astonishment he said sharply:

154

"Do not be a little fool! Why should you marry the Marquis under those circumstances? There are many men who would offer you a far better deal."

"I do not . . . know what you are . . . saying," Ina replied.

She looked again at the Prince, thinking he was speaking so strangely that perhaps he had had too much to drink, but that was something which was hardly likely to have happened so early in the morning.

Then she knew he was concentrating on something different, working things out in his mind, until he said:

"My valet tells me that your uncle came back unexpectedly last night, and now I am beginning to understand. When did the Marquis propose to you—if that, in fact, is what he did?"

The way he spoke made Ina frightened.

"I do not . . . know what you are . . . saying," she answered, "and you have no right to ask me these . . . questions."

She would have passed the Prince, thinking she must get away from the Orangery and go back, as she had intended, to the Hall to find out where the Marquis actually was.

But when she tried to pass him, the Prince put out his hands and laid them on her shoulders.

"Answer me," he said. "Tell me when the Marquis asked you to marry him."

Ina thought it would be undignified to struggle and there was no reason why she should not tell the truth, so she replied:

"He told Aunt Lucy that he wished to marry me

155

and she came to my bedroom last night, to tell me the wonderful news. While she was there, as you have heard, Uncle George returned and she told him too."

"So that is how it happened," the Prince said. "It is what I might have expected! And you, because you are so innocent, were made a 'cat's paw' to pull their chestnuts out of the fire!"

He spoke almost violently, and now Ina struggled against his restraining hands.

"I do not . . . know what you are . . . talking about," she cried. "Please let me . . . go."

She tried to move, but the Prince held her captive.

"Now listen to me, Ina," he said. "I knew as soon as I saw you that I had fallen in love as I had never expected to do at my age. But I love you, and I am asking you to marry me."

For a moment Ina thought he must be joking. Then as she looked up at him she realised he was serious.

"It is . . . very kind of you . . . Your Highness," she stammered, "and of course . . . I am deeply honoured . . . but as I have already told you . . . I am to marry the . . . Marquis."

The mere statement brought a radiance to her face that the Prince could not help but recognise.

"How can you be so damned stupid?" he asked angrily. "Can you not understand what happened?"

Ina looked at him in bewilderment.

She could not think what he was trying to say. She was only uncomfortably aware that he was still holding her prisoner, and they were alone in the Orangery.

"Please . . . let me go . . . Your Highness," she said. "There is really . . . nothing more to say."

"There is a great deal," he replied, "and I will not let you go until you have listened to me. I want to marry you! Does that mean nothing to you?"

"How can it," Ina asked, "when I have already told Your Highness I am to marry the Marquis? I love him and he loves me!"

"Did he tell you so last night in your aunt's presence?" the Prince persisted.

The tone of his voice seemed almost to rasp across Ina's mind, and for the first time she had an idea of what he was trying to say to her.

"What . . . do you . . . mean?"

"You must face facts," the Prince said. "The Marquis is not in love with you, but with your aunt. Can you be so blind as not to realise it?"

"That is . . . not true!"

The words were only a whisper.

"Of course it is true," the Prince asserted. "The whole party was arranged for her and when she came to your bedroom last night saying that the Marquis wished to marry you, I would bet everything I possess it was because she realised your uncle had come back unexpectedly and was likely to discover what she was doing in his absence."

Now at last Ina was aware of what he was insinuating, and even as she parted her lips to say that it was ridiculous and of course the Marquis was not in love with her Aunt Lucy, she began to remember things she had never thought of before.

Almost as if a picture was forming in front of her eyes she could see the door into her uncle's dressing-room open and Lucy coming through it, looking exceedingly beautiful, wearing a blue négligée which Ina had seen before and thought was the most attractive garment she had ever imagined.

And as she moved towards her Ina had seen the blue, almost transparent nightgown that went under it and which she had admired when she had seen it laid out by Lucy's lady's maid on a chair beside the bed.

Ina could feel the heaviness of the Prince's hands as they gripped her shoulders and she felt as if they, rather than the words he used, forced her to go on seeing the pictures which were unfolding before her eyes.

Aunt Lucy in her nightgown and négligée coming swiftly towards the bed, and behind her, walking more slowly, the Marquis.

As Ina thought about it now she realised there had been something about him that had not seemed quite right, and as if the Prince's hands forced her to know what it was, she remembered that his tie had been crooked.

Then Aunt Lucy had sat down on the bed to take away her book and tell her that the Marquis wanted to marry her, and Ina could remember how she had felt!

The ceiling overhead had disappeared and there was the sky and the stars, and a radiant light shining through it, that was not from the moon but a light that came from God Himself.

She remembered how the wonder of it had enveloped her and she was conscious of nothing except the Marquis and his eyes looking into hers.

Then Uncle George had walked through the door which led from the dressing-room and Aunt Lucy had exclaimed with surprise at seeing him.

They had not expected him back and in fact he had said that he would not return until the following day, and yet here he was, a few moments after Aunt Lucy and the Marquis had come into her bedroom!

The Prince was watching her face and as if he knew without words what she was thinking, he said:

"Now do you understand? Now do you see that you have been duped and made use of? Marry me, Ina, and let your aunt keep her precious Marquis and make a fool of your uncle if she wishes, but not you."

He seemed to Ina to paint a picture so horrible, so appalling, that she gave a cry of sheer horror that seemed to echo around the Orangery.

With a convulsive movement of her body she struggled free of the Prince's restraining hands.

Even as he tried to grasp her saying: "Do not go, Ina. Listen to me!" She ran through the orange trees and out into the corridor.

Then she was speeding frantically across the Hall and up the stairs, quite unaware that the servants looked after her in surprise.

If there was anyone in the passage as she ran to her bedroom she did not see them.

She only ran faster than she had ever run before, to the only sanctuary she knew.

She pushed open the door and saw Hannah bending over a trunk that was half packed.

At the sound of her entrance the old maid straightened herself. Then as she saw Ina's face she began:

"What's the matter? What's happened . . . ?"

Ina flung herself against her, putting her arms round her neck to cry:

"Take me away, Hannah! Oh . . . take me away! I cannot . . . stay here! I have to go . . . somewhere else . . . anywhere . . . as long as I need never . . . see him again!"

Then as Hannah's arms went round her she burst into tears, but even as she sobbed, she repeated:

"Take me away . . . hide me! I cannot bear it . . . I cannot stay! Oh . . . Hannah . . . Hannah . . . take me away . . . !"

Chapter Seven

INA WALKED out of the Villa and into the garden.

It was high up in the hills above Nice and there was a panoramic view of the islands, the sea and the very blue sky.

She stood looking at it, then as if it hurt her she turned to where among a huge clump of flowering shrubs there was a stone seat.

She sat down, putting beside her the drawing-book which Hannah had suggested she take with her into the garden.

"Go and draw the view," Hannah had said commandingly. "It's what your father would have wanted to do and it'd be hard to find a better one."

Ina knew she was speaking the truth. At the same

time, she had no wish to draw, and the new book which Hannah had bought for her in Nice remained empty.

Even to look at it made Ina remember another book, her old one in which was the drawing of the Marquis, but she had not opened the covers since they had left Chale.

Hannah had understood what she felt and saying very little had taken her away, as she had begged her to do.

She had known by the way Hannah spoke and by the expression in her eyes that she was aware of why the Marquis had asked her to marry him, why Aunt Lucy had brought him into her bedroom.

To Ina it was not only that she had been thrown down from the heights of ecstasy into a slough of despair, it was also that she felt dirty and besmirched by what had happened.

She was very innocent and she had no idea exactly what a man did when he made love to a woman, but she knew that her mother had loved her father deeply and ecstatically, and that any other sort of love must be wrong and wicked.

Aunt Lucy was married to Uncle George. She was his wife. She was also old, older than the Marquis, and to Ina the whole secret intrigue was revolting and unclean.

"I c—cannot see them again," she sobbed, "and I . . . cannot look at them or . . . speak to them."

Hannah had understood.

With the efficiency she had learned from looking after Ina for so many years and being for the last few of them both mother and father to her, she had somehow managed to arrange for a carriage to be waiting at a side-door to carry them and their luggage to the station.

She had naturally not said that Ina was going with her, but sent a message by another servant to say that Miss Ina had a headache and would not be coming down to luncheon.

She added, to make sure that nobody came to see her, that Ina was sleeping.

Holding on to Hannah's hand because her eyes were swollen with crying, Ina had slipped down the side staircase and out into the carriage, after the luggage had already been loaded onto it.

There was only one horse and one man on the box to convey them to the station, but they caught an early train to London before anyone was aware they had left Chale.

It was Hannah who knew from which station they could catch a train to Dover, and Hannah who without even asking Ina, took them both back to Nice.

When they reached the town where Ina had lived with her father and then with Mrs. Harvester, the warmth and the golden sunshine made it seem as if they had stepped into another world, but she could feel nothing but her own unhappiness.

When she could talk a little more sensibly she realised how clever Hannah had been in bringing her to the one place where she had money.

All the money Mrs. Harvester and her father had left her was still in the Bank in Nice and Hannah had not reminded her to ask her uncle whether it should be transferred to England.

So it was there waiting for them, as was the furniture which they had stored with Roland Monde's pictures, when they had set off for England.

It was Hannah who had been certain that once he learnt where Ina was, Lord Wymonde would think it his duty to bring his niece back to England.

"Now listen to me, Miss Ina," she said two days after they had arrived and were staying in a quiet *pension* to recover after the hot and tiring journey.

"What is it?" Ina replied listlessly.

"I thought today we'd go and see if we could rent a Villa," Hannah replied.

She thought there was a slight glint of interest in Ina's eyes, but she did not speak and Hannah thought it would be difficult to recognise the happy, radiant girl who had found Chale an enchantment, and its owner the man of her dreams.

"What I am considering," Hannah went on, "is what we should call ourselves."

Ina looked puzzled and she explained:

"Sooner or later your uncle will think it likely that you've come back to Nice. He's your Guardian and, if he wishes you to go back to England, you'll have to go with him."

Ina gave a little cry.

"No, no! I cannot do that! I will not go back . . . I could not . . . bear it!"

There was no doubt that the idea frightened her and Hannah was aware that it would be a very long time before she could get over the shock of what had happened.

"What I'm going to suggest," Hannah said in her

quiet, practical voice, "is that we change our names. We'll try and rent a nice little Villa high up in the hills outside Nice, and there will be no one, if we have different names, to connect us with either Mrs. Harvester or your father."

Ina clasped her hands together.

"That is clever of you, Hannah, and we have enough money to stay there for years, if nobody finds us."

Hannah nodded.

"We'll stay, at any rate, until you feel you can face your uncle again. After all, he's done you no harm."

"He has always been kind to me," Ina said in a low voice, "but he would make me return to England, and I could not speak to . . . Aunt Lucy."

"Now there's no use in dwelling on such things," Hannah said briskly, "and what you've got to do, Miss Ina, is to come with me to the Bank and draw out all the money you have deposited there."

"Why should I do that?" Ina enquired.

"Because they know who you are, and if we continue to use that Bank, they'll have our address."

"Of course!" Ina exclaimed. "How clever you are, Hannah!"

"There're other Banks in Nice," Hannah said, "and we'll deposit the money in another one under our new name."

"What do you suggest it should be?"

Ina found it amusing to choose herself a new identity.

She decided that it would sound more respectable if Hannah was her "aunt."

She laughed at the idea of "Aunt Hannah" but thought she would make a very much nicer and more . . . respectable aunt than her real one.

There was no need for words.

She put her hand over Hannah's for a moment and it told the elderly woman how grateful she was and how much she loved her.

"Mrs. Walgrave" and her niece Ina found there was a large choice of Villas to rent if they were prepared to pay.

They hired a carriage to drive them up into the hills, and finally chose a Villa further along the coast beyond Villafranche.

It was small, but the garden was beautiful, and even Hannah was obliged to admit that the view was fantastic.

Yet once they were settled in, arranged the furniture Mrs. Harvester had left her and hung her father's pictures on the walls, Ina found the very beauty of the garden and the view made her think of Chale and the Marquis, and her whole being seemed to ache with her need for him.

She knew that never again would she know the ecstasy she had felt when she had believed that he loved her. When his eyes had met hers as he stood at the end of her bed she had felt as if he had swept her up into a starlit sky.

But all the time he had loved Aunt Lucy and, as the Prince had said, she had been used as "a cat's paw," to save them from Uncle George.

Sometimes when she lay awake at night, Ina would think that she would go mad as what had happened repeated and repeated itself over and over in her mind, so that she could not escape from it.

Then she told herself she hated the Marquis for what he had done to her, but the tears would flood to her eyes so that she cried despairingly into her pillow because she would never see him again.

"What will become of me?" she asked now, as she looked out over the sea.

She was too intelligent and sensible to think that she could stay here with Hannah forever.

And yet while she had no wish for friends or acquaintances, she was well aware that it would be impossible to contemplate a lifetime with only one person to talk to; one person to be with.

Besides, Hannah was old, and sooner or later she would be left alone.

"I must use what talents I have," Ina told herself, "and that way keep busy."

She knew the only thing she could do was draw, but she thought that perhaps she could find a teacher in Nice who would instruct her in the use of oils so that in time she might become an artist.

But when she looked at her father's pictures she knew he had a touch of genius which she did not possess.

She could not explain what it was, and yet undoubtedly it was there. As for herself, the only thing she could produce that had any real merit was her drawings, and those were often so personal and perceptive that she was afraid of them.

She kept thinking of what had happened when she drew the Marquis and she had the frightening feeling that if she picked up her pencil, whatever else she tried to draw, the result would be him: his face, his arms, his hands . . . his lips!

"No, no, I dare not even try," she told herself.

"There must be something else I can do," she thought and tried to concentrate on "something else."

But inevitably all that filled her mind was Chale, and round it, through it and over it, the figure, the face, the eyes of its owner.

It was as if there was nothing else in the whole world but him, and as if now she realised her loneliness without him, Ina put her hands up over her eyes.

"What am I to do?" she whispered. "Oh, God, what am I to do?"

She heard someone approaching and thought quickly that Hannah must not find her crying.

The old maid was trying so hard to make her happy and Ina felt ashamed that she could not respond more easily to what she tried to do for her.

She took her hands from her eyes and wiped away the tears even as Hannah reached her and she heard her stop just behind the stone seat.

"I am afraid you have caught me day-dreaming . . ." Ina began to say in what she hoped was a light tone.

She turned her head as she spoke, then was very still.

Standing behind her was not Hannah, but the Marquis.

At first she felt he was not real, but just a figment of her imagination. She had conjured him up so often that it was difficult to know where her thoughts ended and reality began.

Then as she stared at him, holding her breath in case he should vanish, he said in a deep voice:

"Ina!"

The name seemed to be wrung from his lips as if he could not control it.

She thought there was a light in his eyes, but she could not be sure of anything, except that he was there.

"Your maid told me this is where I might find you," he said after a long moment.

"Hannah!" Ina gasped.

The Marquis's lips twisted.

"She tried very hard as 'Mrs. Walgrave,' to tell me she had never heard of you, but I saw your father's signature on one of the pictures in the hall."

It was impossible for Ina to speak, she could only stare at him as if to make sure he was really there.

Then as he walked to the front of the stone seat and sat down beside her, Ina turned her face away to look out over the sea.

For a moment the Marquis just sat looking at her little straight nose, the soft mouth which drooped at the corners, before he said quietly:

"You made it very difficult for me to find you."

"H-how did you . . . find me . . . ?" Ina began, then she gave a little cry. "Uncle George . . . he is not . . . with you?"

The Marquis heard the note of fear in her voice and said quickly:

"No, I am alone. Your uncle was convinced you were hiding somewhere in England, but I had the

169

feeling you would come back here, where you lived with your father."

Ina did not speak and he went on:

"I tried to use my mind perceptively, as you told me to do, to find you, and now I have succeeded."

There was silence, then at last Ina spoke.

"W—why should you...want to find me? Please...go away...I wish to be left...alone."

"That is what I expected you to say," the Marquis answered, "but Ina, you cannot mean to punish me more than I have been punished already!"

He drew in his breath before he went on:

"This last month, when I thought of what I had lost I knew that my life would be utterly empty and pointless unless I found you again."

Ina wanted to reply that he had Aunt Lucy, but then she knew not only that it would be a vulgar thing to say, but also she could not bear to speak of her aunt.

As if he understood what she was thinking the Marquis said quietly:

"I want to explain so many things to you, but it is very hard to begin."

At last Ina could find her voice.

"There is nothing to...explain," she said quickly. "I just want you to...go away."

"I think if I did so, you would reproach yourself for the rest of your life for hurting someone who was desperately in need of help. And no one else except you, can understand the agonies I have passed through."

"What...agonies? I do not...understand."

The Marquis was silent for a moment. Then he said:

"Actually I doubt if there are words to express what I am feeling now, and you will have to use your perception—the perception that you told me about, and which frightened me when we sat together under the almond trees."

"You were . . . angry with . . . me," Ina whispered.

"Not angry—frightened," the Marquis corrected. "You made me see how much was missing when I thought my life was complete and almost perfect in its own way."

He paused before he added:

"You pointed out new horizons to me, and at first I was appalled at having to leave the security I knew for the insecurity you suggested."

Despite not wanting to understand what he was saying, Ina knew exactly what he was trying to tell her.

"You are very young," the Marquis went on. "At the same time you have lived a very different life with your father from that of most young girls. You must therefore be aware that a man has two sides to his nature—a higher and a lower. It is inevitably a woman who offers him the choice."

Ina gave a little shiver.

As he spoke she was thinking of Aunt Lucy's beautiful face and seeing her, not as she had done before as a relative, but as a Circe enticing the Marquis away from all that was highest and best in his nature.

"You must try to believe me when I tell you," the Marquis continued, "that I have never in my whole life met anyone like you before, and I swear I had no idea what love could mean until I saw your eyes and the expression on your face when you were told I wished to marry you."

"How . . . could I have been so . . . foolish as to . . . believe it?" Ina said bitterly.

"It was and it is true!" the Marquis declared. "Ina, I am asking you to believe something that seems incredible. Yet at that moment when your eyes met mine, across the bed, I knew that I loved you as I have never loved a woman before, and that you and only you could carry me up towards the stars."

Ina started, because it was what she thought herself had happened.

She clenched her fingers tightly together in her lap and told herself she should not listen; that he had come into her bedroom with Aunt Lucy who was wearing only her nightgown and her négligée!

How could he do that and talk to her of a love that could carry him towards the stars?

She knew even as her mind argued against it that her body was quivering because there was a note in his voice that she had longed to hear, and she was afraid that if she turned to look at him she would see it in his eyes.

"I love you, Ina!" the Marquis said quietly. "I know now I loved you that first evening when our eyes met across the dinner-table, but I did not believe what I felt. And I loved you when I saw you

172

dancing under the almond trees, and thought that nothing could be more beautiful, more perfect, and that you were the enchantment of spring."

He gave a deep sigh.

"That is what you gave me—an awakening of spring in my heart. But I was too stupid and too selfish to grasp at it because I was afraid you would upset my comfortable, well-ordered life in which there would be no changes, but only a continuity of boredom until I died."

"That is . . . what you . . . want."

"It was not what I wanted even then!" the Marquis argued almost aggressively. "It was what I had grown into and what I had. It was only you who were able to see there was so much else that was different and far preferable in every way."

Ina did not say anything and after a moment he said softly:

"I am begging you to forgive me."

There was a plea in his voice which she found difficult to resist, and yet without turning to look at him she managed to shake her head.

She did not see the expression of fear and despair on the Marquis's face. Then after a long pause he said:

"I want you to do something. It will not be very difficult, and if you have any feeling for me at all, you will do as I ask."

"What is . . . it?"

"I can see your sketch-book lying beside you. You told me what happened when you drew me once before. I want you to draw me again."

Ina did not move and after a moment he said:

"Please, Ina, it is not very much to ask."

Because she felt as if he compelled her, she picked up her drawing-book and held the pencil in her hand.

Then as she opened it and looked at the blank pages she had the terrifying feeling that she might draw something horrible and perhaps obscene.

Supposing, she thought wildly, she drew him with Aunt Lucy in his arms? Supposing she saw his handsome face not as it was, but gross and deformed?

Then she felt as she had felt so often before, as if while she held the pencil in her fingers she had no control over it, and it started to move of its own volition, and she decided she would draw the Marquis's face as he wanted her to do, and he would be satisfied.

Then as she started the Marquis said very softly:

"Forgive me all my sins,
Forget the past, our life begins
Together and for ever - Yet
My love is deeper, stronger and more true
Because I took so long in finding you."

He spoke the words very slowly and it took so long that she had almost finished her drawing before it came to an end.

Then as she realised her eyes had been half-shut and she had not seen what she had drawn, she felt a sudden fear, and turning for the first time to look

174

at the Marquis she put her left hand over the drawing without looking at it.

"Do not . . . look," she murmured.

"Why not?" he asked. "I am not afraid, Ina."

The way he spoke meant so much more than the words, and now his eyes held hers, and it seemed to her as if everything else in the world vanished.

She sat looking at him and he at her for what might have been a few seconds or several centuries of time.

Then he said again:

"Forgive me. I have written a dozen poems on the way here, all asking you for mercy, and yet now I only want to say over and over again how much I love you!"

As he spoke Ina felt as if a surge of joy moved through her like a phoenix rising from the ashes, flying from her heart to her breast, sweeping away the misery and despair of the last weeks.

She started when the Marquis said in a different voice from the one he had used before:

"Let me see what you have drawn. If I have failed to reach you, then I am prepared, if you want me to, to go away."

Ina looked down. She felt him draw a little closer to her and because he was waiting, very slowly she lifted her hand from the book.

The drawing was very clear, but it was not the Marquis's face as she had expected, but instead there were the mountains as she had drawn them once before.

But there was no sign of the pilgrim sitting by

the roadside and for one second Ina thought he was not even included in the picture.

Then she saw him: not where she had expected—a figure at the bottom of the mountain—but almost at the top of it, and as she looked a little closer she saw that he was not alone.

There was someone beside him, and she knew it was herself.

She heard the Marquis give a deep sigh that seemed to come from the very depths of his being, then she felt his arms go round her, and he said:

"You understand—or rather, your adorable, entrancing mind does! We are together, my darling, climbing the mountain and when we reach the top, there will be another mountain beyond it."

He pulled her closer still and her head fell back against his shoulder. Then he looked down at her for a long moment before he said:

"I love you with my whole heart and soul!"

His lips were on hers and to Ina it was as if the Heavens had opened and he carried her not towards the stars, but into the very heart of the sun.

She could not believe that, in what seemed the passing of a minute, she had been swept from the misery and despair that had encompassed her like a dark cloud ever since she had left Chale, into a glory and a wonder that was almost too ecstatic to be borne.

She knew, as she had always known, that when the Marquis kissed her they would become not two people but one, and she would be an indivisible part of him as she had been meant to be since the beginning of time.

She felt herself tremble with the miracle of it and

felt the Marquis was trembling too.

Then there was love like the leaping flames of the sun burning away her unhappiness and all that was wrong and wicked.

Love and more love, until it was impossible to think, only to feel. . . .

———————◆◇————————

The Marquis raised his head and looked down at Ina to say in a voice that was curiously unsteady:

"I love you, my darling. I love you until there is nothing else in the whole world but my love for you. If you send me away, then you will destroy me."

"I love you . . . too," Ina said, "but . . ."

"Forget it," the Marquis interrupted. "There is nothing in the past that need concern us. It is only the future that matters. The future, my precious little love, in which you will show me the way and it will be different from anything I have ever known in the past."

He smiled as he said:

"I have so much to tell you, but for the moment I only want to kiss you."

He pulled her closer still.

Then he was kissing her with long, slow, passionate kisses that grew more insistent and more ecstatic until Ina felt not only that her eyes were blinded by the glory of the sun, but that the warmth of it flickering through her, moving upwards to her lips to meet the fire which she sensed burnt within him.

"I adore you, I adore you, I worship you!" he

cried, "and I also want you as I have never wanted anything in my life before. How soon will you marry me?"

It flashed through Ina's mind that perhaps they should wait before they got married, then she knew there was no point in doing anything so unnecessary.

They belonged to each other, they were already, through the Blessing of God, one in their minds, their hearts, and their souls, and a service of the Church would make very little difference except that she would bear his name.

Once again he knew what she was thinking, and he said:

"I thought a lot before I found you and, in fact, I had many long sleepless nights in which to do so."

"You have not . . . yet told me how you . . . found me."

"It is immaterial now that I have," he answered, "but I visited every hotel and *pension* and then every Estate Agent in Nice once I learned that Mrs. Harvester with whom you had been living before you came back to London, had left you money which your uncle told me had not been transferred to England."

"That was clever of you," Ina said with a little smile. "Hannah was quite certain that nobody would ever be able to find us."

"I think no one would have, except myself," the Marquis agreed, "and that was because I felt all the time I was seeking for you, that you were drawing me like a magnet. There is some vibration between us, Ina, which neither of us can deny, and which even when we are apart shines like a light in the darkness."

Ina gave a little murmur of happiness. Then she said:

"When I was thinking of you and longing for you, I used to feel that perhaps you would be . . . aware of my thoughts and how . . . unhappy I was."

He pulled her closer still.

"You will never be unhappy again," he said, "and, my darling one, I am relying on you to show me the way to the top of the mountain, and to the new horizons which lie beyond it."

"That is what I want to do," Ina whispered.

"Shall we start by exploring a very different world from the one I have lived in up until now?" the Marquis asked.

She looked at him enquiringly, and he explained:

"Have you forgotten I have to find inspiration for my poems, and perhaps even to write a book?"

Ina gave an exclamation of astonishment.

"That is what I thought you should do."

"So your mind put the idea into mine," the Marquis said. "I am quite prepared to do it, my lovely one, but only with your help."

"You know I will help you . . . you know I will do . . . anything that will make you . . . happy."

"Then that makes it very easy," the Marquis replied. "We can be married tomorrow, or the next day. Then we will have a very long honeymoon; a honeymoon in which we will lay the foundations of our new life which will support and sustain us when we have to return to our responsibilities in the old."

Ina knew exactly what he was trying to say to her and she knew, because she was close in his arms and against his heart, that once they were married, nothing in the old world, not even Aunt Lucy, could hurt them.

She could see Chale almost as if it was a vision, enveloped in sunshine, and she felt as if the almond blossom was once again falling around them and imprisoning them with an enchantment which no one could break or spoil.

"That is what our love will be," the Marquis said as he watched her eyes, "and we will not return home, my precious one, until the almond blossom blooms again next spring."

"Where will we go?"

"Wherever you take me," he answered. "The world is ours, and we will explore it hand-in-hand, like pilgrims, and I have a feeling it will enrich our minds and our souls so that we can both of us give something to the older world which it has needed for a long time."

"That is . . . what I want to . . . do," Ina cried. "You are so clever and so . . . magnificent, and Chale must stand for everything that people . . . look up to, and . . . admire."

"As you inspire me so will you, my lovely, sweet darling, inspire them," the Marquis replied. "How lucky, how very, very lucky I was to find you!"

She smiled and for a long moment he looked

down into her face as if he would etch her beauty forever in his mind.

Then slowly, as if by hurrying he would spoil the perfection of the moment, his lips found hers and he was kissing her somehow in a different way from before.

Ina knew it was because he dedicated himself and her to everything that was the highest and best of which they were capable.

It was something which they knew would be revealed to them when they reached the horizons of love.